FIFE COUNC~~...~~
LIBI

C12

Morley Book

F   £6.99

CE

GW01460010

Dedicated to the memory of my dad, Leonard Fox
1914 - 1997

"What you got to tell me?"

WITHDRAWN FROM STOCK

Derek M. Fox is a creative writing tutor and lives in Chesterfield, Derbyshire. He has had short stories/articles widely published in the UK and abroad. His first novel, the very popular *Recluse*, was first published in 1996 and reprinted in 1997.

by the same author

Recluse

DEMON

"The soul of man is larger than the sky,
Deeper than ocean, or the abysmal dark
Of the unfathomed centre."

Hartley Coleridge

'Gavin, don't!'

Jane Lennard slapped Gavin Pountney's hand away and folded her arms. This she didn't need. His smirk was secondary to her pause. She listened, unsure —

Yards away a seagull's wings beat the air; below the cliff, the sea chattered on the shingle.

Jane shrugged, niggled by Gavin and whatever had forced that other feeling. 'I suppose you think I'm just another notch to your ego.'

'Bull. Twenty-one and never been kissed. I've heard about you and Tyler being an item...'

Jane sat rigid, senses attuned... but to what exactly?

Behind her the path disappeared amidst tall grass to where a signpost leaned like a crazy drunk. She thought of Jerry Purdy, quite why she wasn't certain. Perhaps it was because Mattie, his niece, was marrying Nick Tyler tomorrow, and that really hurt.

'...a bloody tease that's you.'

'Gavin, shut up.' Wide blue eyes locked on him, her sarcasm apparent. 'You love to hear yourself. Other opinions don't matter.'

The air hummed and Jane fidgeted, an unheralded chill forcing her to tug a heavy cardigan about her shoulders. She stood, her handbag tipped, contents scattered.

On the point, the lighthouse beam danced across darkening water; to the right swaying lights pinpointed the jutting finger of Tibb's Cove's only pier. She derived little comfort from either, unease like an unwanted lover — like Gavin.

'What the hell's wrong with you, Miss Prim? Still got the hots for Tyler.'

His words went unheard as she tried to penetrate the gathering gloom. It hadn't been a sound, she argued, more a sensation. 'A stirring of air,' she whispered.

'What are you on about?' Gavin's long, narrow face creased in a gargoyle grimace. 'Head in the clouds, Jane. What with poetry and amateur dramatics you've no —'

He fell quiet, both of them stupefied at a huge, indefinable shadow rolling in some thirty feet above the chopping waves.

Arthur O'Connell winched his boat up the shingle towards his cottage nestling in the lee of the cliff. Six lobster pots clattered on the jetty, Arthur's neck hairs bristled.

His Irish ancestry was a joke: he didn't believe in the little people. At seventy-six, with a war behind him, he felt that right now he should be in THE TRAWLERMAN supping his first of four nightly pints of Guinness.

'Holy Mother, it can't be.'

From the cottage door, O'Leary, his black Labrador, howled, and cowered.

Johnny and Charlie, the ten-year-old Sheridan twins, raced across the flat beach towards the rocky promontory of Macey's Nose.

'Beat you this time, Johnny boy,' Charlie yelled.

He was five yards ahead, bike tyres cutting new veins in the sand. They raced against their own limits and the encroaching twilight. And hadn't Frank, their dad, encouraged the competition? 'Better than littering street corners. Only your two selves to protect.' He was right, for the late Eighties smacked of a new darkness, a change in the order. Frank had told them, not in so many words, but they knew what he meant.

The wind shredded Charlie's shout, that same wind a harbinger of something coming in from the sea. Charlie skidded, aware Johnny wasn't following, flung sand peppering saltwater pools. 'JOHNNY, COME —'

He bit off the words to stare at what his brother stared at; at what Jane and Gavin were seeing; at what O'Connell could not believe...

It's a movie, flashed through Jane's mind. But if so, where were the camera crews? Years ago, but not now. Tibb's Cove offered no welcome.

Gavin thought: Fucking crazy. Not seeing...YES I AM.

O'Leary's howls downgraded to a frightened whine, O'Connell's guts threatened, and he hadn't even had a drink. Charlie Sheridan winced from the fall off his bike, his ankle twisted under him, wheels clacking to a stop. Johnny ran towards him. No seabirds cried. The air was static, fresher, and the sea resembled an oil painting, full of life, yet lacking it.

And horror came in on the landward wind...

...slowly at first, limping in at a tilt, her four engines silent, only two propellers spinning. Sun glinted from the mid-upper and for'ard gun turrets, Browning 303's jutting up and out like damning antennae. Shrapnel had torn away one wing tip and a tail fin, her heavy underbelly shredded, the red white and blue roundels still defined in dying light.

Gavin broke the church silence. 'Oh mother... it's... a Lancaster Bomber!'

In a flashback, Johnny Sheridan saw the model plane his Grandad had constructed as it spun slowly on the wire suspended from his bedroom ceiling. But this one was *real*.

O'Leary crawled beneath the upturned boat, muffled barks calling a master who raced down the shingle, O'Connell unable to accept an inevitability he had known must come. 'But it can't come back... IT CAN'T. God, Mel, please don't do this.'

Lower now, undercarriage up, a grey-black silhouette of camouflaged wartime colours, the number RF 499 emblazoned on the rear fuselage, bomb motifs tattooed beneath the salt encrusted cockpit housing.

'It's her,' O'Connell said, as the massive shadow beat a way in, blinding light screaming from the cockpit canopy, the Brownings first burst rupturing the shingle before tearing him nearly in half.

Blood and disbelief stained his face, one hand tore the air, the other clutched O'Leary's lead in dead fingers.

The twins ran, Charlie's limp a hindrance, the plane banking, drumming towards them. No sound, every sound. Picture memories of Grandad's photographs flashed across their minds, as they staggered towards the breakwater, and the bulk of Macey's Nose.

A stitched pattern of disturbed sand headed their way.

'CHARLIE, RUN.' Johnny knew his Dad would never forgive him if something happened to Charlie. He dragged him, yelling across puddles, to the sanctuary of the breakwater. Woodchips flew, a sharp splinter gouging Johnny's cheek.

A silver moon courted the sunset, and Gavin Pountney watched terrified as the bomber climbed, moon rays lighting the cockpit and death sitting there. *Death* in a leather flying helmet, goggles and sheepskin jacket... *Death* returned from God knows where.

Gavin yanked Jane behind the rocks, the onrush of air a

torment, because it was the only sound there was.

Jane screamed. From the shore, O'Leary lamented.

CHAPTER 1

Jerry Purdy shivered in the cooling night, wondering what in hell he'd seen fly past the moon. To the left of the poplars, and just to the right of swaying prom lights at the end of the narrow street, the church tower's flag flapped like a derisive handclap.

Jerry thought about Mattie Wells, twenty-eight and finally getting married in the morning. He hummed the tune that would herald the bride, but it lacked warmth. He loathed weddings. Girls mocked him, his size, his manner, but because Mattie was kin he would go, he owed her that much.

Head spinning from booze, Jerry closed the door and staggered to the lounge. Setting his Fosters on the stained occasional table, he belched loudly and aimed his bulk into his Mam's scratched leather chair, only to shove himself back up and hike back the net at the window.

The grass needed cutting. 'Tomorrow,' he muttered. And three gnomes peered from a bank of azaleas and weeds, their over-round eyes scary in the dark.

He remembered being six, when he and his father, George had christened the gnomes Grumpy, Doc, and Dopey. The buggers had remained there since 1944, and Jerry hadn't dared tell George they scared him. He couldn't because

George scared him too.

GRUMPY. DOC. DOPEY. Loveable cartoon characters, but any resemblance to the fairytale ended there and to Jeremiah Purdy they held bad memories.

He belched again. 'I did see something. Not DT'S this time, Fatso. Wonder if Dykes saw it on his way home? Hope he did, then I know I'm not that pissed.'

Him and Dykes had much in common. From schooldays they had shared lives. Secrets, chasing down the same streets, wooing the same girls. 'On'y Dykes was better at it. And taller, *and* slimmer.' Purdy liked girls, but hated himself. He lacked confidence, and fell into the trap that a bottle held better dreams. Sure, he talked about girls with Dykes, they nattered about everything.

'Especially the friggin' war.' And about how they would stand with their parents watching the Lancasters' turn over Macey's Nose prior to heading across the sea to give Adolf a dose of real English cheer. And Dykes, damn him, had mentioned the name. MEL.

'I'll phone Dykes, he's bound to be home. He'll know something.' He chuckled. 'Sod'd see the devil if I told him Old Scratch was sitting on the fence.'

The chair groaned as he settled. He snatched up the phone and punched the digits. He whittled a broken nail with his teeth.

'See you made base, you old fart. What? Oh, sorry Jaqui, thought he'd be home. Eh? Nah, he's been left a good twenty minutes. Tell the old hoss to make contact, I seen something funny in the sky. No, it wasn't a pink whatsit. Yeah, take care. See you at the wedding.'

He stared at the phone. 'Funny, he should be home by now. Isn't fair on Jaqui.'

Dykes thought the world of Jaqui, the truth of it evident

when he had nursed her through that bad car accident. Nearly lost her.

He emptied his can, suddenly aware of how quiet the house was. The can fell to the floor when something scraped the window. He came off the chair like a whale breeching. 'If that's them fuckin' Sheridan kids at it...' There were abstract red marks on the panes.

He loathed kids nearly as much as he did women. His face festered with an anger fed by recent incidents of wheelybins tipped over, his Mam's prize rose uprooted, and by far the worst — a dead cat nailed to the door.

That had scared him. Drunk as he'd been, groping for the lock, he found a tacky, stinking cat and had been forced to use a whole bottle of Domestos on the door, the floor and his fucking shoes. The trousers he'd had to bin.

'Joke is this... hopefully.' Purdy hitched up his trousers and flung back the front door with such force that it cracked the plaster. His great fist punched the air. 'BASTARDS. JUS' LOOK WHAT YOU DONE TO MY WINDOW.'

Nothing moved. The breeze hissed derisively. And Grumpy, Doc and Dopey watched, insufferable grins mocking.

'GODAMMIT.' He rattled his shin on a planter. Blinded by tears he rubbed vigorously at his injured limb, and when he looked up he couldn't quite make out the tall figure he thought he saw by the gate, reflected neon bouncing from what Purdy was sure were — 'Goggles?'

He slammed the door, shot two bolts and turned the key. As an added precaution he hooked on the safety chain. The name *Mel* branded inside his head like a neon sign. He sweated, but felt chilled to the bone. 'Damn you, Dykes. You and that bloody airfield. Jesus, we were fifteen...'

Leaning on the door, his tone held that awful edge of hysteria brought on by silly talk and booze. 'Yeah, sure, that's it. I'll sleep on it… Aw man, there was no plane tonight. Didn't see any aeroplane.'

But there were noises, Jerry. Dull slaps, remember? And the whining? Dykes said it was like bullets ricocheting in one of them cowboy films you like to watch.

They had looked at one another, burst out laughing, and supped some more.

Edging away from the door, Purdy convinced himself he had heard the noises again after Dykes had waltzed up the path. *They reminded him of* that *night*.

Double checking the locks, he drew a sobering breath and waddled down the hallway he knew, in the house he knew. The carpet runner, the faded print on the wall, the coat stand, even the skimpy posy arrangement his Mam had placed on the small table before she'd left to meet God, all were familiar. But not comforting.

He mopped his brow with a handkerchief, his breath laboured, trapped now in a hothouse of his own sweat. Behind him the door eased, a creak invading the pregnant quiet.

'CHRIST!' Purdy became entangled in his own feet as someone scrabbled at the opaque glass, a pallid, drooling face there, and gone in a blink.

In the lounge it was at the window, beyond the nets.

Purdy hugged the wall, one hand gripping the veneer peeled sideboard. His Mam's photo smiled at him. 'Why can't you be here, Mam? Tell it to go away. Light the light, Mam. Don't like the dark. Tell me nice stories. Not like the ones Emmy tells.'

And Mam would. She would stroke his brow and sing: 'When you wish upon a star —'

Soothed, the lyrics floated around his mind, along with Goofy, Donald Duck, Mickey… and GRUMPY, DOC and DOPEY.

'Jesus, not them. Dad you put 'em there. YOU TAKE 'EM

AWAY.'

But George couldn't. Everyone had gone. Purdy was on his own.

He knew something had invaded which didn't belong: something his sister, Emily had pushed at him until he believed and was terrified of it.

The airfield. A mile away.

Going through the wire, Jerry? Into the airstrip? Going to find Mel 'cos Emmy says so. Dykes leading, you begging him not to go, 'cos you knew there was something real bad in the hangar...

He edged towards the phone. 'Dykes gotta be back.' Punch the numbers. Yeah. 'Shit.' Again. 'Lord, there's no fuckin' dial tone.' Or comforting signals to assure him of a real world out there. But there was... something.

Whispers. And laughter. Crazy sounds. From a gaggle of men. Sounds crawling all over the house, and terrible, freezer centre temperatures like at the abbatoir. Sounds like the ones he'd heard at Hatcher's Field.

'Find Mattie. Mattie'll know what t'do. Mattie'll chase 'em away.'

There were voices in the static, and laughter, the rumble of trucks, someone calling: 'MEL. MEL,' above the noise, the heat, the engulfing incandescence...

HATCHER'S FIELD, 1954.

Eyes closed against insufferable images, Jerry Purdy flung the phone and heard it shatter on the edge of a glass fronted cabinet. Mam's best nick-knacks tumbled. Then some prat screamed from beyond the window: nails raked the glass, the blood smear more evident. Purdy viewed the apparition through splayed fingers and screamed: 'DYKES. LORD GOD, WHAT HAVE THEY DONE TO YOU?'

The window cracked, top left to bottom right, a gurgling, choking noise eroding Purdy's last resolve.

He wished he was at work in Franklyn Moon's factory off the bay. What matter Moon was a shit, it was a job, he got paid, and he could play cards behind the packing cases. Won a bit, lost a bit at Solo, Brag, 'Happy-fuckin'-Families.' Anywhere had to be better than here.

Or crawling through the wire?

'MAM, I DON'T LIKE WISHING ON STARS ANYMORE.'

Resurrected childhood fears ranted, especially where the dead walked, and an old airfield threw out dares to anyone foolish enough to crawl under its wire.

'Christ, what did we tap that night?' Purdy asked. His flesh rippled, fear wringing him out. He looked at the window again, the gurgling had stopped, but suddenly Dykes' bloody dead face crashed through the glass, a hand tearing at the curtain, his body thrown about like a toy without batteries.

Purdy threw himself into the hall as bullets sliced yard long strips from walls, the door and Mam's chair. He scooted up the stairs as fast as his bulk would allow and locked himself in the bathroom.

He listened. The night growled.

There were no stars to wish upon. For Purdy, darkness lived, and real fear walked inside it, that and loneliness his real enemy?

The steady drip of a bath tap intensified: he tried to think of the wedding, of something tangible through the booze. And the fear. 'Yeah, the wedding. Me an Dykes'll have a high ol' time... Aw, hell Dykes, why'd you have to go and get dead?' A tear rolled down his fat cheek.

Shouldn't have gone in the hangar, Jerry, my son. It was George talking. His father as ever was, but that... 'Is impossible.' They were there, you know. Three of 'em. LANCASTERS.

Jerry's mental banks threw out disjointed thoughts about

how that Yank Flight Lieutenant christened the bombers. And
the Yank knew his old man. 'An' I can't forget the friggin'
names 'cos they're outside, in the garden. Shut up. STOPPIT!'

He had to leave, get out. And face the man at the gate? 'Isn't
nobody.' Keep telling yourself that and just get the hell out.

On the landing he peered into shadows, the numbing cold
forcing a rigid, one step, two step lumber down the stairs. He
wished the Sheridan twins were to blame, that he could cope
with. In the hallway he touched the dried flowers, trying to
gain a residue of a mother who had protected him, but these
flowers were as brittle as her dead bones. Quietly, cautiously,
he eased the bolt back, took off the chain and turned the key.
And forgot the planter. Purdy hit the lawn hard, and screamed
as his left wrist snapped, the bone-crack like a gunshot.

Drizzle dampened the pathway, the gnomes polished by
damp, and watery neon.

Lurching towards the gate, he looked back. The torn body of
Dykes dangled from the window, dark blood welling from a
mess of blue-black punctures, his silver hair thrown out like
two grim horns.

Purdy turned away, swallowed bile and tramped down the
cobbled street, every step pain-wracked, his vision blurred by
rain and tears. 'I don't believe in dreams.' His words cannoned
off rows of cottages whose curtains stayed closed. 'Help.
Mattie, where are you?' Tom Sheridan? 'Find Tom at the shellfish stall by the pier.'

Jerry, it's past midnight. Talk sense.

Pain came in waves, rain intensified, the sky sooty with
cloud. The church clock struck the quarter hour. A blue strobe
guided him to the promenade, its gathered crowd, paramedics
and police. The Sheridan twins were there, talking with a
heavy set sergeant. He could tell the guy about Dykes...
'Somebody shut that whining dog up.'

O'Leary nuzzled a black body bag as the paramedics lifted it into the vehicle.

Everybody seemed strangely subdued, like the crowd at his school sports day when he'd fucked up on the shot put.

He was dimly aware of some pathetic singer in HATTERS NIGHT CLUB belting out the old Vera Lynn standard 'We'll meet again'. Franklyn Moon owned HATTERS. 'So what, he pays good. All power to him.' Purdy regretted the thought. Too much power can be dangerous.

Giddiness and multicoloured lights disorientated him. Through the haze he saw Nick Tyler in close proximity to a dark haired girl whose pale face wore fear the same way he did. 'Tyler shouldn't be doing that. He's marrying Mattie tomorrow... today...' He bit down on his pain as he tried to focus on the girl leaning into a policeman. She shouted a name: 'GAVIN.' Heads turned. No-one answered, except the dog, his howls nerve-wracking.

'Please somebody... shut the bloody dog up.'

Wind whistled up the street, the ambulance pulling away, siren wowing. It drowned the dog, and it wasn't half so bad. And the figure dressed in flying gear standing in the entrance to HATTERS threw Purdy completely. George?

Turning, incomprehension weighing him like a brick, Purdy slumped in a bus shelter, garbled pleas lost as he slid slowly off the seat.

Nick Tyler saw him. Fat Purdy, the guy always giving advice to Mattie — interfering twit.

Debating what he should or shouldn't do, Tyler argued that his own life was messed up enough. Something had to be done about it. Twenty-nine was no age to curtail his lifestyle. He had a job in computers starting Monday, but with Jane Lennard still buzzing around, and him marrying Mattie Wells, his name wasn't in the Cove's top ten right now. Thankful Jane had gone in the second ambulance, Nick nudged Purdy with his foot eliciting a groan.

'Can't leave you here, old lad.' Straining with the effort, he heaved Purdy onto the seat and satisfied he'd stay put, wandered across to the phone booth outside the night club. He waited until another ambulance collected Purdy before he shot up an alleyway to disappear through a dark doorway over which a fortune-teller's sign flashed scarlet in the night.

CHAPTER 2

'Dearly beloved, we are gathered here in the sight of God and in the face of this congregation —'

Mattie Wells studied the vicar.

'— join together this man and this woman —'

He has light eyes — like Reverend Black when you were four, Mattie? Dad said never to trust anyone with light eyes. Black had cold eyes. Uncle Jerry said to forget it. Think about the wedding, your day. But where is Uncle Jerry? He promised.

It's nice and cool in here. Mattie bowed her head, the coronet of flowers irritating her skin, too tight about her close cropped dark hair. If I keep my eyes on the vicar, she told herself, I won't have to see past him to the vestry door.

Like the day at the Church Garden Fete when Black tipped Strawberry Cream Soda all down your white dress. He told everybody it was accidental didn't he? And that sickening, condescending smile of his won them over, right?

Recollect? Yes you do. You were running between the tents and the White Elephant stall because Dad had promised you a drink of Pop, the money clenched in your tiny fist, your giggles bouncing off the tent walls — until you saw the shadow. Scared you it did. And no, it wasn't Black, you know it wasn't.

Nor was it Mum or Dad, in fact it wasn't anyone you knew.

And the smell, like something you had never experienced before, but afterwards you recalled the time the drain had been blocked at home. You told your dad: 'Like the grate outside, Daddy, when you had to get the men in to clear it out.'

The shadow on the tent wall elongated, it sort of climbed up, way up, to overpower you and everything: it overlaid the church and the yews, and despite the sun's warmth — really hot that day — you puzzled why it was dressed in a leather sheep-skin coat. *And* why you ran back the way you'd come when it said from behind that funny mask it wore: *'Take my hand, Mattie, come and see the big aeroplane'.*

They had model planes on the Bring 'n' Buy stalls, but you knew even then, that there wouldn't ever be one big enough to get the shadow in. So, you ran from it, and when you looked back there was nothing there. The lady at the refreshment stall, all teeth and smiles and blue rinse, said: 'There you are, poppet, one Strawberry Cream Soda just for you.'

The second you turned and started to walk away your mouth dry from the heat, and the slight niggle you couldn't be rid of, you stopped dead, along with over one hundred other souls. Weird sounds echoed over the loudspeakers hanging from their poles around the vicarage garden... Funny, squawky, metallic shrieks, like a radio was out of tune.

'Due to atmospherics I'm sure,' Reverend Black told the throng. 'Nothing to worry about. Soon put it right.' And didn't he seem to glance towards the gap in the tents you had just vacated?

The people had stood as though frozen, their rapid eye movements questioning, especially the older ones, *the ones who remembered*.

Somebody said: 'It's like a repeat performance.'

Another said, 'Aye, like its every ten, maybe twelve years or so... it comes back.'

They knew then, didn't they? All of them, but wanted to get on with their lives. The music drowned the strident, ear split-ting, teeth grating sounds, and Eddie Cochrane belted out 'Three Steps to Heaven'.

And you cannoned into the Very Reverend Mr. Black who was talking to your mother and a few others. Mother didn't mind one bit when he took your arm, even as Mother tried to wipe off the stain on your oh so pretty white apparel with the bows and frills...The stain. Like blood on snow.

He walked you to the side door of the church, where the sun didn't reach, and you shivered because it was so cold. Yes, Black took you in there, into the vestry to clean it off.

The horror of it stayed, grinding away in lucid moments. If it hadn't been for Dad, and Joanna, I wouldn't have come to this church ever again.

This is your day, remember?

Dad smiled, and nodded, pride suffusing his face.

Mattie looked to the vicar again. He has a nice, deep voice. It washes over me like the tide on a summer day... *Not when you were four. Black's voice was something else again.*

She shook it away. *My day.* And God must be good because this vicar won't let anything nasty happen. Wonder if God is tall like the vicar? I like tall men. Nick's tall and blond. His beard tickles when he... She experienced a pleasurable shudder. And he gives me self-assurance, like Uncle Jerry does.

Why won't Nick look at me?

Anxiety tightened her stomach, her fingers ravelled in the ribbon threaded through her bouquet. The vicar's tone inten-sified. 'And if anyone can show just cause or impediment why these two people should not be joined —'

Mattie moaned, the middle fingers of her left hand bloodless, panic a growing ball...

Black was carrying her, and she whimpered, she wanted Dad. And all the while Black dabbed at the stain with a cloth, trying to clean off the red stain, as he neared the vestry door.

She broke the emotive forces by looking squarely at the vicar. With a yank, Mattie wrenched her fingers free of the entrapping ribbon, flowers scattering across the stone flags. Restless children made noises, parental hands snatched them to order.

Len Wells whispered harshly: 'I'm glad your mother's not here to see this, our Mattie.' His agitation was apparent, despite the pride he'd displayed earlier. Mattie guessed he wanted out of here just as she did. Her dad knew, he remembered.

The vicar loomed above her, his head bobbed, swept back silver wings of hair lacquered, precise. But the eyes were hardly reassuring.

Black had been dark and loathsome, especially when he had pressed her against the stone wall in her underwear.

Strawberry pop? Or blood? On her dress. Pop, or —?

Her personal demon wouldn't quit. It taunted and laughed inside her head. And she could see... Black? NO. NOT HIM. *The other one.* Someone she wouldn't ever forget —

like a deepening shadow overlaying the stone.

It wasn't blood, dammit. It was Strawberry Cream Soda. Then, yes, but later when he...

A baby wailed, and Mattie glanced towards Joanna, her sister's smile one of hopelessness rather than encouragement, her hands folded neatly over a very pregnant belly.

We're all overwhelmed, Mattie was thinking. She sought Nick, reached for his hand only to find it wasn't there, his non-committal shrug accompanying a lacklustre smile.

Jesus help me. Tell me Nick wants me for who I am — ME. Mattie Wells, spinster of this parish and never been... except by... Oh God, and except when I was four. Dear sweet Lord,

I'm twenty-eight and want to be married... DON'T I?

On the wall over to the left, two flags — a Union Jack, and the Royal Air Force flag — fluttered. And over the vicar's right shoulder the vestry door stood open, and Mattie could see herself, the pasty faced child, pressed against cold stone.

The vicar picked up on the confusion, repeating: 'If there is any just cause or impediment... let him speak now or hereafter hold his peace.'

Mattie wasn't conscious of the silence, she was thinking about seeing IT for the first time.

The door stood wider now.

He's in there, his trousers open, IT sticking out and touch... touching me.

The silence wailed. Mattie knew she had to stop the charade. It wasn't right, none of it. Nick was not right...for her. MEDALS. On Mam's dressing table. Her collection.

'For who, Mam?' Mattie had asked only to be ignored. But when Mam had gone shopping, and Dad was setting his seedlings, she had sneaked up to the room and taken a peek at the sepia photo of a smiling airman Mam had kept hidden under her packs of tights. The photo which had scrawled across it: *To EM. Keep it warm. Love Mel.* There had been three kisses.

Mattie had never let on. Secrets. Everyone needs them. Mattie kept hers locked tight. And no-one except herself and Uncle Jerry ever knew the real truth of what happened in the vestry twenty four years ago.

She wrung her hands and stared at the vicar for the millionth time. It cannot be, she pleaded silently. Not here, in this place so defiled before. I cannot marry —'... MARRY MATTIE WELLS.'

Who? She turned to stare at Nick. He looked solemn, and repeated the statement.

At the rear of the church, Jane Lennard gave an audible sigh

and sat down, thankful Nick had kept the promise whispered
to her last night before she climbed into the ambulance.

The vicar leaned towards Mattie, as a verger restrained Len
Wells from tackling Nick. A quiet pandemonium bubbled,
throw away words caught and let go; children shouted; a slap
sounded, it went quiet. Relief flooded over Mattie. She could
be free. Her head swivelled towards the vestry.

*...the child screeched into an empty void... writhed as the huge body
towered above, and a hand, stinking of incense, closed over her mouth
as she lifted the candle, pupils dilating...*

Mattie felt faint. Shrugging off her father's hand, she
dropped the bouquet and whirled to discover she was hemmed
in by the crowd. Jostling them aside, making a way through,
she needed to find her secret self. More, she had to find the
reason she had clung to a faded wartime photograph from
Mam's drawer.

Or did it go even further back... maybe to when she was
four years old?

The cottage. Emily's cottage. Her Mother's place. Yes, I'll go
there, talk to Mam.

Family yelled, kids screamed, the noise somehow over-awed,
the air filled with a deadly drone.

Sometimes things return. Her mother's words.

And the congregation heard the whisper: puzzled, every-one
fell into their own thoughts, rattled by memories they did not
fully comprehend — yet. But if anyone dare ask, doubtless
some of the congregation would say: *'It's coming... AGAIN.'*

Mattie threw herself out of the doors, onlookers and friends
parting, perplexed as she ran to the waiting Bentley. She
climbed in on a rustle of taffeta and breathlessness. 'Driver,
DRIVE.'

Inside the church, the vestry door slammed, the throng
begging the question. The air shifted, the RAF ensign swirled

once. The vicar reached out but could not bring himself to touch it. Folding nervous fingers around the handle, he opened the vestry door and paused, curious as to why the Book of Remembrance should be open on the long oak table when normally it was retained in the knave.

The room was empty, but the vicar courted the feeling he was not alone.

Slowly, he read aloud the names of a missing bomber crew lost over Berlin. He paused at Melville Cross, birthplace Sweetwater, Texas, USA.

It should mean something: it didn't.

And the church, its standing, became as nothing, the man of God dearly wishing he had never taken up the call.

CHAPTER 3

The cup of Quick Brew tasted brackish, Jaqui Dykes nursing her anguish, unable to forget Jerry Purdy's babbling as she had sat by his hospital bed. It had been the only place to go after the grim, stilted news brought by the solemn faced police-woman. Did she believe it? Accept it? News bulletins had been full of an aeroplane shooting up the beach and a few locals. Surely not. Hungerford was fact, but never this.

What was it Jerry had said? Something about a guy in flying gear outside HATTERS. Her answer of: 'Fancy dress party,' had been more believable. All the while she had been wringing her hanky, the vision of Dykes hidden away in a freezer drawer, a name tag on his toe.

Marilyn Gates, a neighbour, coughed, sipped tea and said: 'You look awful, Jaqui.' She drew heavily on a Capstan Full Strength, and irritated Jaqui by rattling a spoon.

'Marilyn, if your hubby had been chopped up by a million or so bullets how the hell would you feel?'

Marilyn pinched a residue of tobacco from over red lips. 'Feel, ducky? I'd probably run up a flag. That one of mine's nothing to write home about.'

Jaqui watched Marilyn titivate her over-lacquered hair, waiting to be amused if it snapped off.

'One thing's certain,' Marilyn said, her gravelly tone razoring at Jaqui's resolve, 'they had to be smashed out of their heads not to realise some pillock in a plane had it in for 'em. I mean Tibb's Cove isn't exactly a designated training zone.'

Jaqui was numb. She couldn't cry and felt guilty.

Marilyn tilted back on the chair, the legs screeching on the kitchen tiles, her over tight trousers stretched like a wet suit across her thighs. Jaqui willed her to leave.

'That Jerry Purdy was always strange.' Marilyn screwed out her cigarette and lit another. 'Ever since that business in the church with Mattie Wells. And then Emily, her mam, flipped and popped her clogs. They've been a funny family.'

'Tell me about it, Mar.'

Marilyn leaned across and touched her hand. 'You tell me.' She poured more tea.

Jaqui sighed. 'Dykes and Jerry were buddies since they could walk. Smoked their first fag together, had their first woman.' She heard herself laugh, a tight, not unpleasant sound given the circumstances. She was sure Dykes wouldn't mind. 'Gal named Sarah Twigg. She married Mike Riggott from the baker's shop near Woolworths.'

'Her? The local bike. She's had more doodah than an oompah band.' Marilyn paused, round green eyes willing Jaqui to say more. 'So,' she prompted, 'what are you gonna do about Purdy? You can't blame him.'

'Mar, talk sense. Purdy wasn't just Dykes's mate. Would I have visited him at the Cottage Hospital otherwise?'

Marilyn's answer was a shrug, a shake of the head.

Jaqui looked at the rain washed window, late Saturday afternoon noise muted beyond the slatted blind. She kept hearing Purdy on the telephone as she had waited for Dykes to come rolling home last night. What had he said? Something that couldn't exist, flying in the sky.

'He never did tell me about that business at the old airbase, y'know.'

Marilyn frowned. 'You talking to me or reminiscing?'

'What? Oh, sorry. Thinking aloud I suppose.'

'Well whilst you're at it, let on about that church business with Mattie Wells.'

'Oh no, that you will not hear from me, Mar. It's dead and buried —' Jaqui gnawed her lip regretting her choice of words.

'Hey, I was chattin' to Marge in the Takeaway about four,' Marilyn said not to be put off. 'She told me there was another rumpus at the church. At the wedding, or rather non-wedding.' She grinned, it looked pathetic. 'That Mattie Wells again, ran away from her own splicin', how's about that? Ran away from Nick Tyler. Oooh, I could make his hair curl.'

Jaqui pushed herself up from the table and went to lean on the sink. Dykes's I HATE MONDAYS mug sat on the drainer. Still she felt nothing.

'Haven't you anything to say, Jaqui?'

Jaqui turned. 'Personally I don't give a shit if the Queen waves bye-bye to all she's got. I've lost my bloke, it's enough.'

'Well, if that's all, I mean if you don't want to listen…' Marilyn smoothed her trousers and pushed the chair a little too aggressively under the table.

'Listen,' Jaqui retaliated, 'is all I ever do where you're concerned, Marilyn. A hotch potch of gossip on legs that's you. And I don't much care if the whole soddin' air force flies past. Just go home, Mar.'

Marilyn feigned hurt. 'I'll put it down to grief, Jaqui.'

'Yeah, do that.'

'So much for my being neighbourly.'

'See you around, Mar.'

The pause seemed overlong, Marilyn eventually whirling, her intended prima donna exit made comic by her high heels skidding on the highly polished tiles.

The quiet following the door slam was welcome.

Jaqui sat again at the pine table, her mind walking down that cold mortuary hallway to stare at the remains of her husband, recognisable only by the ring in the envelope she was handed. Unless she counted his blood soaked driving licence, his credit card neatly drilled, and his membership card for the snooker hall.

Dykes. A name only: of life, nothing but a blood-spattered overcoat punctured and as flat as a car tyre. The ring she'd bought for him in Blackpool on a day trip. A cheapie from a promenade shop. But Dykes, bless him, had treasured it, told her it brought him good luck.

'Not this time, you reprobate,' Jaqui whispered.

And the age difference of eight years hadn't mattered. Jaqui had loved Dykes with a fierce passion many didn't understand. Fifteen years is a while, yet in the words of the song "It wasn't a day too long". Rather the days were too short. Until now.

Seeing a motionless Purdy hadn't helped. Just him and three empty beds in a silent ward.

'Hell,' she said straight out. It had gotten to her. Damn right it had.

Bombers. Dykes dead. She thought of many things, but the one important point was why had Dykes never said a word about Hatcher's Field.

She lifted the teapot, poured another cup, spooned sugar into it, and poured in milk. Leaning over, she tipped the whole lot into the sink. The cup clattered but didn't break.

'JESUS, WHY DYKES?' Jaqui shook. 'WHY DID YOU HAVE TO LEAVE ME? GO LIKE THAT?'

The rain hammered the window, unable to drown the wracking grief of Jaqui Dykes.

Purdy lingered between sleep and a sort of awareness. Semi-comatose through drugs, his left arm throbbed, and he muttered incoherently.

He called out: 'MATTIE,' hating the echo in the dark hangar, the call interspersed with shouting men, trucks rumbling, and clinging to three enormous sleeping behemoths beneath the ceiling floods.

And he was in another building with a shining cross, cold pillars, where moonbeams lit the Roll Call of the Dead, airmen all, who had died for King and Country.

And someone who sounded awfully like his own father whispered: 'You woke us up, Jerry. Always were a meddler.'

Purdy walked the two like a lost soul desperate to be rid of them and muttering: 'Didn't do nothin'. Didn't wake anybody up.'

What about 1954? You meddled then, and that was some meddling, oh boy, was it some meddling.

A chuckle in his inner ear... Three of 'em strangled by weeds, and George, his big Dad telling him not to be daft. 'On'y Plaster of Paris, lad. Can't hurt you.'

Jerry knew different. Dad used to hurt him. And wasn't there someone who would whisper in a Texan drawl?

The garden became a graveyard, the church dwindling, shifting. Emily beckoned.

'*Mam —*' he shouted, '*why didn't you listen. Emmy is rotten.*'

The moonlight scrawled brittle shades across the room. Purdy groaned, straining to lift himself from the warmth, reaching to touch the moon with his good hand, the hand snatched back, fingers iced, crackling with frost.

Should've worn gloves, the sheepskin jacket.

The thought snapped teeth, leaving him wondering why *he* should have done those things.

Mam stroked his brow. She was singing. But he hated the

song now. No stars to wish on. 'I'm here, Jerry,' she said.

'... here. Jerry, please wake up. I have to talk. Jerry, it's me, Mattie.'

Mattie? Thank God. He had called and she was here. He made out her soft features, noted the concern in her dark eyes. 'Mattie,' he blurted, 'it was 1954 all over again. Dykes wouldn't keep quiet. I... I told him it was bad to talk about it. It's Mel, Mattie. MEL. He's back. Jus' like he always will be. Christ, if we'd left well alone it wouldn't be this bad. Not. This. Bad.'

Her hand continued to soothe, and Purdy realised she was the only real friend he had.

Although years separated them, they had discovered a seed which had grown into a common bond. Criticized by many, they kept counsel. Let the others think what they like, he wouldn't harm Mattie, or she him. They used to build sand-castles, and dive into their world — a world where hideous things never walked.

Until Melville Cross insinuated himself into their minds. All because of a fucking photograph Emily wouldn't ever destroy.

Mattie had made her mind up to say nothing about today's non-event, for it would serve little purpose and she argued, probably upset him. He'd wanted her to be happy. Then again, she had no doubt Uncle Jerry wouldn't argue. He had always wanted what was best for her anyway.

The staff nurse had told her not to pay any attention to Jerry's muttering, and Mattie had nodded politely. The nurse couldn't ever know what Mattie knew.

Jerry loved her smile, her touch, but couldn't come to terms with the heavy smell of disinfectant in the room. He tried a return smile, but his face didn't belong. He felt gorged with shame and guilt, guilt over Dykes, and shame because of his own obesity, his manners. He dearly wished he could change, blot out the image, be something he wasn't.

Schooldays had been the worst: name calling, always the butt of cruel jokes and heartlessness carried through by his tutors, and his own father. He felt the tears, and cursed his incapabilities.

Mattie dried them away. 'Jerry, you'll be okay.'

But you can't know what I've seen, his mind screamed, and he gripped her wrist.

'JERRY, you're hurting me.'

Apologies rolled out as he watched her massage the pain away. The rain teemed, a violent, unheralded crack of thunder shaking the window, metal dishes rattling on a trolley by the doors. Lightning dimmed the nightlights in the room and outer corridor, garish light unnerving.

Purdy jolted upright to jab a finger towards the darkened alcove to the left of the doors. 'Who's that?' A shadow, somewhat darker than the rest appeared to detach itself from the wall and step out.

Quiet stitched the room. In the corridor something: a wheelchair? a trolley? A squeaky wheel drew near, and passed by.

Mattie followed his pointing finger, and shrugged. 'I don't see anything.' She picked up his water container, topped up his beaker and tried to get him to drink. He smashed it aside, Mattie startled by the sudden action, but both transfixed by it, as it skittled across the floor.

'I ASKED WHO THAT IS.' His finger gestured wildly. 'THERE, FOR CHRIST'S SAKE. The man in the flying gear, like under the lamp when... when they shoved that poor sod in the ambulance... Aw somebody shut that fuckin' dog up.'

This outburst sent Mattie towards the door to click on the main lights, chasing shadows away. It had shaken her like a shadow on a tent wall had when she'd been four. Turning, her look told him what she was thinking.

'You're right, I'm stupid.'

Mattie said nothing, unwilling to resurrect part of her own secret soul,

With great effort, Jerry came off the bed and wavered for a second or so. He searched the room, eventually slumping back on the bed, face beaded with sweat.

'Honest, I did see it. Please, you have to believe me.'

He looked so lost, so afraid. 'Jerry, I do believe you. We're a team aren't we? We don't tell lies.'

That was a truth if nothing was. Still unsettled a little, Mattie followed an instinct and retrieved an object just inside the doors. Here was proof. Proof Jerry had been right. Her hand trembled as she studied it, eventually holding it out for him to see. Jerry recoiling from it made her shudder that much more.

The carved face might be classed as a lucky token, maybe a talisman. To Jerry, it was a grotesque gnome peering from the azaleas. Something he had seen before. And something he so dearly wanted to forget.

CHAPTER 4

'Joanna's upstairs in her room,' Len Wells said as he straightened from turning on the gas fire. He massaged his lower back. He was tired and at his wit's end, his eyes emphasised by puffy shadows.

Mary and John, Emily's cousins, hovered by the door. John a little unsure, shuffled his feet and looked anywhere but at Len.

'Thanks for coming back,' Len said, 'it helps after that bloody fiasco in church. I had hoped our Mattie might... What's the use? Her decision.' He sat on the edge of an armchair.

'I always said it wouldn't work, didn't I John?' Mary's manly tone was enough for them both. 'Mattie's too much like Emily, proud and stubborn.' She snorted. 'And look where it got her.'

She fiddled with her handbag clasp, and smoothed imagined creases from her floral skirt, the garish colours hardly complimenting her sallow complexion. 'No, it wasn't right. I even telephoned our Mattie, didn't I John? —'

John merely nodded, busying himself with a roll-up, tobacco spilling onto the carpet.

'— Go on, you tell our Leonard that's what I said.'

Behind Mary's back, John winked, and Len offered an imperceptible, yet understanding nod.

Always bloody nagging, Len thought. Ever since she could talk. Why in hell John married it I'll never know.

Wartime, couples thrown together — the common bond. They had both met at the munitions factory, and after a lust-filled one night stand, and years spent regretting that the child of their union had been stillborn, the pain and nagging was chiselled in both faces.

Family, mused Len, who needs 'em? Friends, I can pick.

Politeness had forced his earlier thanks, but he wanted them to leave. There was much to think about, especially Mattie. And the past. Tyler wasn't wholly to blame, Len very aware it took two to tango.

It comes down to Mattie, her wants selfishly out-weighing her need to marry, to be tied down. The church wedding had been wrong, too many memories, especially the day of the Fete. That and Emily. Len knew Mary was right. Mattie was very like Emily.

'Being a father to two girls hasn't been easy, Mary,' Len said. His grin smacked of dissatisfaction. 'One man and three females in the same house. Hardly a proper balance is it? Em's gone, and so has Mattie in a way, and to cap it off, our Joanna's nearly due.'

'Has she said who the father is, yet?' Mary squeezed her heavy backside into a cane chair against the wall. 'I mean I'm not one to harp on, kids do what they like these days, but I'd have thought —'

'No, Mary, she won't talk about it.' Len stared into the radiants on the fire, and felt an abnormal chill. Briefly, he closed his eyes, only to open them quickly, a sudden vision of Emily on the landing, fingers hovering over the handle on Mattie's bedroom door.

Emily Wells, dead for fifteen years, yet still moralising like a member of the Salvation Army.

The gossips had their field day after the business in the church, all of it so much crap. Small towns bred gossip, Tibb's Cove clung to it.

Mary was saying: '... all these presents, what's to become of them?' She had selected an iron from the overcrowded table in the window recess. 'Mine's a steam iron, they're much better.' She read the label. 'From George's sister. Might have guessed. Off the market I dare say.' Her head shot up. 'What have I said about smoking, John?'

'Leave him alone, Mary.' Len felt suddenly protective towards John, reasoning that if he had been given leave from females he was damned sure he wasn't having any of Mary and her belittling. 'If John wants to smoke then fine. It's probably the only pleasure he gets these days.'

'Meaning?' Mary plumped up her feathers.

Len stood. Not a tall man, he still towered over Mary. 'Meaning, if I'd got you, Mary, smoking and drinking would be a welcome diversion. So shut it and go home.'

Len saw John grin, and jettison a long stream of cigarette smoke.

'So,' Mary sneered, 'all blokes together.' Like a fat pigeon she strutted about the room. 'You dare say that to me, Leonard, when we all know what sort of a father you've been to those girls. Emily knew, oh yes. She told Jerry not to interfere, to leave Mattie alone —'

'Mary!' John took a pace, forcing Mary's eyes wider, daring him to say more. He did. 'Shut it, just leave it be, it's past.'

'Don't you interrupt me.'

Len closed his hand over Mary's arm, tendering a meaningful squeeze. 'Mary, leave me to take care of my own.'

John shoved a handbag at her, his face abnormally red, a symptom of the blood pressure which would finally cause a massive heart attack in a few more days. But it would be the shock of what was to come would initiate it. He said defiantly: 'Come on, woman, we're leaving.'

Perhaps for the first time in ages, Mary was speechless. John made good use of his advantage and steered her through the door to bundle her into the clapped out Austin Cambridge.

'You're for it,' Len whispered.

'I think not. Not today anyway.' He finished his smoke and flicked it over the hedge. 'High time I had a bit of a say.'

Len watched the car disappear. Above, the sky was a mass of heavy cloud and garish orange streaks. He closed the door and blinked at his reflection in the hall mirror. 'Fifty-four in a month, you bugger,' he said. Leaning closer he discerned several more unwanted lines on his receding forehead, around his eyes.

Glancing up the stairs, Len wondered if he should talk with Joanna, but decided not to. She needed her privacy: he would respect it.

In the lounge, he reached for his bottle of Black Label from the teak cabinet to the right of the fireplace. Len was particularly proud of the cabinet, the way he had crafted the joints. Just an excuse to be away from Emily for a while, out there in his garden shed, his own private world.

The first drink eased the anxiety, the second took away the chill. Like Santa Claus in a grotto of gifts, he muttered: 'Santa isn't real. He doesn't fly through the skies anymore.'

But something does, Len, lad.

He poured a third.

The normal comfort of the house wasn't there: the warmth was absent, along with love and laughter. 'The hell with it.' Len raised the glass. 'To absent friends.'

He felt warmer now, positive he could get used to this. If only Jo would make her mind up, talk to him, then maybe a part of his own problem might be healed. 'Family! Alone is great.' But he wasn't exactly alone, Emily wouldn't let him.

He took another swig. 'To Em, may you rest in peace, you bloody rotten cow!'

Her ashes were on their dressing table in an overbearing urn, all gilt and tarnished EPNS. It sat by the rack of medals, Emily's air force memorabilia. And all of it down to her eccentricity, Len had told himself, later explained by the growing brain tumour which had seen her off.

He'd listened to the six thirty local news. That Irishman, O'Connell dead; the Sheridan twins chased, and Jerry's mate, Dykes shot to pieces.

'Christ, what the hell's happening?'

Hadn't O'Connell been in the war? Len couldn't recall.

The quiet felt unnatural, and Len spilled whisky over his hand when a small parcel slid off the table.

'Where the hell are you, Mattie?' he grumbled. 'Come home and talk to me. I forgive you.'

His euphoria had been short-lived and he concluded he hated living in this cocoon of non-communication. He vowed he would make it up to both his daughters.

The package taunted. A floorboard creaked, but not from Joanna's room where he would expect. It was from his own room: his and the late, unlamented Emily's.

'I'm ineb... inebriat... Pissed. That'll do.' The room fogged, he blinked, and groping, collected the package.

Puzzled, he read, and re-read the tattered, dog-eared card tied to the coarse wrapping paper. 'Surely this isn't a wedding present.' It wasn't.

The card said: **TO LEN**.

'Mattie. It's from Mattie. Always one for little jokes, our Matt.' Too damned right.

From upstairs, a slow, methodical tread ran from right to left. Still gripping the package, Len stalked to the hall door and shouted upstairs: 'JOANNA, THAT YOU?'

Only the pacing came back.

Len closed the door and leaned on it. 'Emily,' he whispered, 'not again. Why can't you leave me alone?'

Tearing open the parcel like it was the only thing to do to get his thoughts off her, he stepped back as an object fell from the package and bounced on the carpet. On one knee, and about to reach for it, Len Wells shied away from the abhorrent leer on the face attached to the cracked leather key fob. The card still in his hand read:

HATCHER'S FIELD OPEN DAY
JUNE 19TH
A REUNION

Len went on fast freeze. Two days away. Images soared. *A mist choked the clipped precision of barbed wire, the humps of air raid shelters contrasting with the greater bulk of silent hangars, an admin block, and a squat control tower. In the silence the slap of a windsock in a rising breeze. A running figure and arms reaching to gather it in, to protect it from the evil emanating from the open hangar doors — an evil which choked even the nettles sprouting from cracked tarmac...*

the image fading now (who had it been?) *becoming Mattie racing down the church aisle, torn clothes, congealed blood, and him calling, screaming her name, Emily's name, all the time attempting to catch Mattie, tell her it was all right... but it wasn't, not anymore, the gesture* down the years, *futile.*

Arms folded on nothing, sobs wracked him and reminded him of the empty life he'd chosen — correction, the empty life which had been forced upon him, because... because...

'I lacked the courage to get out.'

From where though, Len? Here? Or the Field?

Presents tumbled piecemeal about him, and the grim face from the key fob stared, even as names tumbled down his mind, down the years.

Comic book characters which George Purdy had told him about, him and Jerry, and Dykes when they watched the planes climb over Macey's nose. And Em' would read the comics, like they all did, as kids.

But out of them all, as though specially chosen, three names stuck. And one other. Ever since the night they trespassed on Hatcher's Field.

Len Wells gripped his glass and swallowed hard liquor.

From upstairs, Joanna screamed.

CHAPTER 5

He went rigid, the demon face leering from the fob, yet more than that, the invitation to the airfield had fazed him more than he cared to admit. Good men had flown from there during the war. 'Aye, and bad,' said as he raced upstairs scared at what he might find. Surely the baby wasn't due...

Len Wells blamed the Field, Franklyn Moon's silly notions and his experiments. He was angry at their own childish whims, flexible minds somehow distorted by a crazy.

Why had Jo screamed? He stared into a hallway the colour of pitch, the air itself penetrated by static, white noise given over to —

'D — *Dopey, course three one zero requesting permission...*' Hiss. Crackle. '*Engine out. Repeat engine out. Bombs not jettisoned. Repeat...*'

The cadence was intrusive, the crackle rising, fading, drifting from where a suggestion of moon backlit burgeoning clouds, and where blue lightning carved an avenue between them.

Len clung to the banister, a sickly smell of kerosene, and sweat, and cordite eddied in waves. A cold wind whistled through rents in the fuselage.

He hammered the bannister, the pain hardly felt. 'WHY DID WE GO THERE?' And then, through gritted teeth, he answered, 'Because Moon dared us, that's why.'

Emily's laughter became a dull reminder. And her chanting: *'Little Miss Muffet sat on her tuffet, eating her curds and whey. Along came a Grumpy, and he wasn't Dopey, 'cos he frightened you aaalll away,'* whittled at his fast dissipating courage.

He took a deep breath, fear replaced by a loathing for Emily, and for what she had done to this family. He went into the room. The EPNS urn sat on the dressing table, only feet from the bed. The rack of medals collected light from the landing — just an empty room with familiar things.

'Joanna.' He pushed her door, it stuck, so he pushed again, harder. The impetus forced him to skid on a slip mat. Arms cartwheeling, Len eventually stopped before the dressing table and faced himself in the mirror. Temporary immobility held him, breath rasped in his throat, a sudden lack of oxygen making him light-headed.

Behind him was Joanna, still in her wedding finery, her skirts hiked up. Sweat glistened, her head threshed, expletives scalding the air as she gave birth. And the shade of Emily grinned, her sackcloth face exuding evil triumph.

Len felt the whisky sour in his throat. From high above the rooftops, the sound climbed in unending fury, and Len caught a glimpse of Melville Cross leaning over the bed, encouraging... laughing...

What came out of his daughter's body met Len with eyes he knew from Jerry's garden behind the azaleas: its fingers flexed. It was the same image from the key fob which had slipped from his own trembling fingers.

His 'N-O-O-O!' hardly destroyed the power invading this room, the house, and not least himself.

The child writhed, the umbilical cord stretched to the limit, lips curling in a toothless sneer, the eyes holding Len Wells from beneath its bloody caul.

Even as it reached, Len threw a bottle of perfume hard at the mirror, the whole surface sent crazy.

In the sudden quiet, Len heard Joanna. 'Daddy —' she panted, 'get the Doctor. The baby's coming.'

He couldn't turn, he dare not, afraid of what he had seen, of what he would see.

Pictures of pop groups were blue tacked to the walls; an array of teddy bears and dolls; the wallpaper bubbled from a months old leak he hadn't yet traced; a rosewood wardrobe sat sedately in the far corner adjacent to the bed.

Nothing moved, clapped, cheered or laughed, Len's relieved sigh a welcome sound. He held Joanna and prayed she hadn't become a part of the darkness invoked by her insidious mother.

Len didn't see the DFC on the floor near the wardrobe, the one which had been the pride of Emily's collection; the one awarded to Melville Cross, of Sweetwater, Texas.

CHAPTER 6

Johnny Sheridan threshed in his bed, his words indistinct, a tracery of blood dampening the plaster on his cheek. Rain drummed the window, the room a wash of light and shade, the swaying model Lancaster tormenting his sleep.

Across from him, Charlie slept soundly in his own bed, the room crammed floor to ceiling with books, models, sports equipment and comics.

Johnny moaned. He could not get back inside the room. Candyfloss clouds prevented movement; lightning danced, thunder rolled. Here was the Laurel and Hardy film he'd watched with Charlie on that video his Dad had fetched. There was a picture on a wall in a house, Stan and Ollie (Johnny and Charlie) running scared as the picture of the death's head stared down... *at him* from black eye sockets... with one difference, this one wore a pilot's hat and goggles...

Words tumbled: *Getchya next time... getchya... time... time... time...*

The quilt entrapped him like bandages around a mummy: it became the bonds of the rustler about to be lynched, the entrapping grass preventing someone he could see running, screaming from Hatcher's Field — someone he recognised.

A guard house reared from the mist, a flaking white rail and rotten wood… the protesting finger of a red and white barrier pole jutted skywards… there was thunder.

That same thunder cracked over Johnny Sheridan like it did over Purdy in his hospital bed. And was the very same Len Wells heard when Joanna's baby made its first push for freedom.

The twins' room was strobe lit as lightning flared, the Lancaster swayed, the air displaced. Over in the corner, next to the cricket bat, their Grandad's old flying boots toppled; from the chest of drawers a clutch of wartime photographs slid, some floated to the floor. And distorted voices, rising, desperate, charged the very air in the room —

'D-Doc calling control. JU88 on our tail. Guns frozen, engine out, casualties. Coming down… Eighteen thousand… sixteen… twelve. Second engine stress. Shutting her down. Repeat, shutting down. Don't think we'll make it. Control? CONTROL? For Christ's sake I can't… Something has the stick. SOMETHING… PURDY!… Coming DOWN.'

Johnny's yell forced him from the bed, the quilt sliding. 'DAD!' he shouted from the landing, 'DAD! DAD!'

Frank Sheridan's eyes flew open. Hurriedly, he clicked on the bedside lamp, the bulb flickered.

'FUCK IT,' he shouted after stubbing his toe on the bed leg, and wished to hell Marie was still here to take her turn. Had she ever? All a mistake when she'd found herself pregnant. Twins! The balloon had really gone into the stratosphere then.

For eight years Frank Sheridan had coped on his own, except on the odd occasion his Dad helped out. Thankfully, Frank had held a job. The local council had been good and whenever house repairs were needed, and potholes appeared, Frank would be on call. He could have gone self-employed with Dykes a few years back, and all the big houses in the Mannon Beach area — including Moon's — would have yielded rich pickings. Moon's cronies didn't worry their heads about trivialities like money.

It was Moon, and close proximity to the man, which had put Frank off, although he did occasionally enjoy a night out at HATTERS. The latest addition to the dancing troupe who resembled Monroe, had winked at him. Things were looking up. A bit of female company would be a-okay, take his mind off other problems. A few games of Blackjack had won him sixty-three quid. That and the girl had to be a good omen.

'DAD!' The dancing girl shimmered and disappeared, and Frank limped to the door wishing Johnny would quit it.

The impetus winded Frank as Johnny threw himself at him. 'Don't let 'em get me, Dad, please.'

Over Johnny's shoulder Frank could see Charlie sprawled out asleep. Above him the model swayed.

'John, hush up. There's nothing bad in here.'

Johnny wouldn't have it, he attempted to read the truth in Frank's face. 'Lemme sleep in your bed. Can't go back in there.'

In. There. It held a sinister undertone.

Frank sat on his own bed cradling his son. 'Bad dream, eh?' Perspiration clung to Johnny's head like cling film. His pyjamas were wringing wet. 'You coming down with something?'

A policeman had brought them home. 'No cause for alarm, sir. Playing on the beach. Lad took a tumble.'

Frank had learned more from Charlie. 'Should've seen it. Came in low across the beach.' He'd made a sweeping movement with his hand. 'The guns were firing, making holes in the sand, bullets pinged off the rocks.'

Frank had been more interested in Johnny's silence, his son's only apparent interest being the mug of hot chocolate. He ruffled Johnny's hair. 'Tell me about the dream, kiddo.'

(Marie, you bitch, why did you leave?)

Johnny jabbed a finger towards the still swaying plane.

'Yeah, I thought so.'

Johnny yelled again, arms thrust out like he was preventing an attack of some sort. 'Move it, Dad. TAKE IT AWAY.'

Forcing Johnny's arms down, Frank managed to calm him, but the noise had brought a curious Charlie shouting that now infamous word: 'DAD.'

'Back to bed, Charlie, John's had a bad dream that's all.'

Johnny lashed out again, catching Frank a stinging blow across his right cheekbone. Frank staggered, upright he still held his delirious son, and carried him back to his own bed. 'Hush up, Johnny, no dream. It's okay.' He wrapped him in the quilt.

The harsh breathing, Johnny's vacant stare; good word *vacant*, described him to a T. And his voice sounded like that of an old man. It threw Frank.

'It came... came at US, Dad,' Johnny was rambling. 'I saw him running—'

Him? 'Who, John?'

'— he was scared. There was somethin' after him. An' he was wavin' like crazy, his jumper caught on the wire. DAD, IT FLEW WITHOUT SOUND.'

Frank felt his short hairs bristle, his scrotum disappear. 'Saw who, John? WHO?'

Johnny stared, and Frank gazed at the grey shadow above them. It's a toy, not a threat, he kept telling himself, but deep inside himself, he wasn't too sure.

He didn't get anymore from Johnny, and that made it even more puzzling.

The hot tea was sobering in the cold light of early morning. It was Sunday, god dammit, the day to lie in. But the brutalising dream of Johnny's filled Frank with a terrible unease.

Should he call Tom? Not a bad idea considering he needed his Dad to explain it away.

And yes, Frank had succumbed, let the twins sleep in his bed, their own door well and truly shut. In fact he'd come pretty near to nailing the bloody thing shut.

Now, with the first real light of day squaring up to the windows, Frank shook his head in disbelief. 'What in hell am I doing? My kid dreams and here I am like Mother Teresa thinking the bogeyman's in the bloomin' closet.'

He knew it wasn't just that. It seemed so real. And it was a problem he had to face for the sake of his family.

Shoving back the chair, Frank reached for the phone and dialled Tom. Outside, the dawn was blood red.

CHAPTER 7

In the aftermath of the thunderclap, Len Wells found the DFC.

Frustrated and angry, he stalked across the landing to his own room, the overhead light collecting Emily's photo, her smile, the tight perm, the over-applied make-up. He had a sudden desire to smash it, to crush her memory, yet held back.

Her face smacked of secrets and held the beginnings of the tumour which would feast on her brain.

The urn's sheen had faded: the empty space on the medal rack mocked. It was her archive of memories, constructed carefully with hands which, after Mattie had been born, had rarely touched him, with one exception.

One miserable day when the wind had been cold off the sea, and Len had been sitting in the fading light of the afternoon nursing a bitterness he hadn't then been able to understand. Emily had pushed and goaded, bringing up Mel Cross, all she had meant to him and him to her. Len had snapped. He had dragged her down and taken her by force there on the lounge carpet, trying desperately to drive out the past which he knew in that fatal, shuddering moment of climax, was tearing them apart.

Emily had screamed, hit him, but the brutal union had seeded Joanna.

Len raised the urn, and never taking his eyes from Emily's picture, he said through clenched teeth: 'You heartless bitch... Let that Yank rot.'

The urge to scatter the ashes became a joy. Dementedly, he said: 'I could suck her up the Hoover and chuck her in the trash.'

His mirror image liked the idea, but he couldn't. A spark of respect still clung. Besides, he had a duty to Mattie, to Joanna. Len replaced the urn, and the medal, wondering just how it had gotten to Jo's room. Maybe Joanna had taken it there, but why?

Unlooked for truth surfaced through the topsoil of his mind, a dread which absorbed rational thought. He was scared, scared of the dark, as pictures of ugly clarity formed. Hangars, dead grass, a control tower filled with moving shadows, voices. Airmen flying off into an unknown... returning bringing only decay and death...

Yet despite it all, Len Wells guessed that the Reunion about which he had been foretold, would exorcise the evil which had plagued this town for so long. If there was a God in this Heaven, it had to. IT HAD TO.

Gripping the jamb outside Joanna's door, Len was sickened when he saw the real truth. Her skirts were hiked up, the bedding soaked in blood. Her fingers flexed towards the thing between her legs, the thing which moved, and breathed, and it reached out towards Len from beneath its bloody caul.

Joanna mewed like an accident-flattened kitten, her skin drawn tight, eyes protruding. For eight and a half months she had carried this, feeding it, nourishing it, her own life force drained by it.

The baby slid on mucous, the cord stretched to its limit. And all the while, Len Wells suppressed the need to tear it free and destroy it.

Joanna clung to him, her tone barely audible. 'Daddy... it shouldn't ever have been... born.'

Blinded by tears, Len reckoned this was his punishment for the way he had seeded his youngest? God help me. 'Jo,' he said, 'don't talk, save your strength. I'll get the doctor.'

He wiped the tears on his shirt sleeve. Is this my lot for denying Emily what she wanted, demanded? And what of God's law? He thought about the church, and Black, and what had happened to Mattie. 'How much more? HOW MUCH?'

He tried to pull away from his dying daughter.

'The child...? What is it?' Her pained eyes held him, a reminder of the lost time he had lived through, solace from a bottle hardly the antidote, salvation in any form, never there.

He couldn't look at the baby, or answer. To him it was a sexless thing lying there in Joanna's blood. Prising his daughter's fingers away, Len stumbled out and towards the phone in the hall.

Each step was a thought: it was a Pandora's Box of evil re-opened; old stories repeated by Emily; barbed wire singing in a callous breeze...

He punched the digits. He'd managed to gabble the address when the lights dimmed, from upstairs Joanna screamed out for him. But she was blind to him when he reached her. She stared into the corner by the wardrobe, towards the material-ising shape. And she said, 'CALL IT MEL.'

In the distance, sirens.

From the gathered gloom, dripping, gelatinous hands reached towards the infant, grasped it and held on, a sibilant: 'Ah,' captured in the air.

Barbed wire strummed, a shred of wool danced from it, and beyond, in the lee of the huge hangar, shapes gained substance. All garbed in airmen's fatigues, tight skin stretched across bony skulls... A gathering...

Len recognised the ring on the hand holding the distorted, pathetic newborn: it was the same one he had placed on Emily's wedding finger thirty-five years ago.

The word *reunion* repeated in his mind, as he crawled on all fours from that room, hardly daring to look back.

But look back he did, and written in the condensation on the window were the words: YOU KEPT IT WARM.

In that same dawn Frank Sheridan looked upon, Len Wells swore the phrase was written in blood. Bile rose, alongside a vicious heartburn. He barely made it to the bathroom. Sirens blatted, neighbours shouted, and someone hammered on the door.

'Call it Mel,' he said scornfully. From the gulf inside him, the past swirled in unabated terror.

CHAPTER 8

Purdy had requested and got the mobile telephone, the retreating nurse's rubber-soled shoes on the polished floor irritating.

Mattie had left, had said she would contact him back at his house. 'But I daren't go back to the house.' Crazy thoughts strummed weird, awful tunes — thoughts of the night, of Jaqui Dykes, of the wild, stupid things he had uttered just wouldn't let go, and he felt ashamed.

'Get back to reality, that's what.' He clutched the phone, his palm sweated, a sickly grin worn like a scimitar moon. 'Has it ever been normal in The Cove?' And his mind told him again that they should have left things well alone that night in '54. It kept repeating, because he just knew that for some hideous reason they, all of them who had gone that night, had acted as a catalyst for something truly evil to re-emerge from the hell to which it had been consigned.

Sure, Jerry had heard, and read about the top secret experiments at Hatcher's Field, and he'd like to think those experiments had destroyed the plague of Tibb's Cove forever. And it was a plague, no doubt about it — a soul-destroying plague that should never have been conjured up in the first place.

'Fuck Moon, and all he stands for.'

He dialled Jaqui's number. From his cabinet the key ring leered. He two-fingered it. The ringing persisted. Across from him, bedding shifted. He craned to see. It had stopped raining.

'Whatisit?' The drunken slur burped in his ear.

'Jaqui, it's me, Jerry. Jus' wanna say sorry about… well, y'know. I dunno half of what happened. We supped too much that's a fact. It weren't Dykes' fault he went and got hisself shot. One minute we were jawin', then all hell broke loose. Some idiot starts shouting over a radio. Not real, Jaqui, none of it —'

But it is, you wally, else Dykes wouldn't be dead. And what about that fiasco on the Prom?

Jaqui told him to calm down. 'Nobody's blaming you. Time for crying's done. But why Dykes? Does Hatcher's Field tinkle any bells?' The pause told Jaqui she had struck a nerve.

'I searched every draw and suitcase in this house,' she said, 'even the shed out back. I found Dykes's memento box and some clippings dated June, 1954. There's some report about a body found at the airfield, at the bottom of a disused air raid shelter's steps.'

Sure I know, Purdy thought, but I don't wanna talk about it. Nor remember them fucking initials M C.

'Who wrote the report, Jaqui?'

'Doesn't say. It reads: "The decomposed body of an airforce pilot was found at the foot of Number Three shelter's steps. No identification was evident, and foul play is not suspected. Forensic teams are working on attempting to identify the subject. A spokesman for the RAF stated: We are completely at a loss —"'

Purdy hadn't heard most of it. But one word had stuck. *Decomposed.*

The bedclothes on that second bed shifted again.

Jaqui was saying: '— sitting here feeding myself gin, waiting for Dykes to breeze in as he does. So, I'm still thinking how come he was blasted to nothing, only a label to tell me it was him?'

DECOMPOSED. Illuminated lit like the HATTERS sign; it winked like the sun off a perspex canopy. Lord, where had that thought come from?

Jerry's head pounded with the past. 'All your fault, George. Yours and Emily's.' He hung up the phone.

Jaqui held the phone for long enough. 'Silly devil, always blames himself.' She finished her gin, and poured another, raising her glass towards Dykes's picture grinning at her from the open album on the bed beside her.

Raising her glass again she said: 'To keep out the Jack o' Lanterns.' And laughed. It was an old phrase her Mam used to ward off the inexplicable creatures who lived in the darkness. Where? She thought, out there, or in our heads?

'Here's mud in your eye, Mam, wherever you are.' Jaqui slurped, burped and reached for a cigarette. 'If Dykes were here he'd kill me.' Dropping her voice a couple of octaves, she mimicked: 'Smoking in bed isn't right, Jaqui.'

'Yeah, Dykes.' She stubbed it out, fantails of smoke wafted away with her hand.

She nursed Dykes's pillow, and thought about Emily Wells nee Purdy, strangely uncomfortable at the intrusion. Links had been forged between herself, Dykes and Purdy. Her accident, the hovering between life and death, the things she had seen cavorting and laughing hysterically in her coma, and *the meetings*.

Jaqui chewed her knuckles, vaguely recalling snatches, glimpses of the other side. Life after death? 'No, just bloody dreams.' Positive about that?

And Marilyn harping on about Mattie Wells. 'What on earth

had the rape of a four-year-old girl have to do with airfields and bombers? 'That fiend Black committed suicide. And Jerry couldn't sleep nights after it happened.'

The gin bottle wavered, her eyelids weighted. Her hand hovered over the ashtray, checked her cigarette was ground out. Clinging to the pillow, Jaqui slid down the chute of sleep mumbling Mattie's name, yet awful scared to go where dreams took her.

Purdy fought sleep, the bedclothes suffocating. The sedative brought by the night sister about as useful as a boiled sweet, his mind overburdened by thought. Silently, he hummed Mam's old song and soon shut up. Praying didn't help either. But above all, it was the loneliness which became his worst enemy.

Breathing — not his own — intruded, a heavy sigh issuing from the bed opposite.

Purdy blinked, the half-light revealing: 'It's empty.'

Not on your sweet, fat butt it isn't, Jerry, lad. You got company, boy, real homespun company.

And as sure as daylight eased between the blind slats, the bedclothes reshaped into something he recognised, a shape from the dark, from the azaleas... from a sepia print. Jerry tried to shout, his throat had closed.

Draught? Windows are closed, doors are shut. It defied logic.

The sheets writhed, and Jerry was a boy again, listening to Emmy's tales.

It twisted, then bent, like a man stretching under the covers, the sheet trapped arms reaching to take him back into the night-time horror of Hatcher's Field for a repeat performance... On to a place Emily had always said existed: the place where lost souls cling to the rafters of their way in life... Or where priests usurp their calling, driven by restless spirits like… like…

'Grumpy, Doc and Dopey.' And an airman, Jerry. DECOM-POSED. All the way from Texas, a lazy smile beguiling, a root beer held between flexing fingers, his tanned, boyish face a real turn on for the ladies, but the eyes as cold, as hard, and as brittle as coal.

The voice. Recall it, as a boy? 'I'll be back, you sonsabitches. Bet your sweet asses.'

'He can't.' Oh no? Who was it shot up Dykes? The others on the beach? *And tried to do for you at the same time?*

He was *here*. Dead, stinking, yet alive, coming towards the bed, grinning that same grin behind his dirty silk scarf. Gloved hand grabbing the key ring, retreating.

Purdy shouted, long and loud, dust motes flying amidst sunbeams through the tall, narrow windows. The bedside table tipped, orange juice flying, liquid pooled on the floor. Purdy skidded, fell, and crawled towards the trolley. The doors beckoned, and he shuffled along, the floor cold on his bare buttocks, the spectre grinning behind its goggles and scarf.

Should've pressed the emergency button. He was angry with himself, giving in to the fear like that. 'Nothin' there, dear Christ, nothin' there.'

Using the trolley for purchase, he regained his feet and found himself in the corridor, his injured arm slamming the door jamb, his cry lost in the emptiness.

His mind played hide and seek, Purdy scared he might never be able to find himself.

The doors behind him thankfully stayed shut. A footfall fetched him round, and he backed away from the wrinkled hag walking towards him carrying a blood-soaked bundle. From it a baby cried.

Ma told me, Emmy was touched with the devil. I believe that now. Mattie, tell it to go away.

'SHIT. MOVE. GET OUT.'

The child wailed, its keening cry locked forever in the walls of his mind. *Like a four-year-old screaming...*

Forced to return to the room, still uncertain as to where the woman and child had gone, he grabbed his clothes from wire hangers. The place was empty, but it hadn't been, because when Purdy looked, the key fob had gone.

He burst into the corridor and half ran, half walked towards the blue doors a mile away. He dropped a shoe. 'Leave it. Just get the hell out.'

At the doors, he shrugged out of the gown and scrambled into his clothes. His shirt sleeve tore as he tried to yank it over his plaster. 'BALLS TO IT.' With shirt flapping, buttons unfastened, he started down the stairs.

And paused.

Someone unseen preceded him, their passing fouling the air. *Like a blocked drain.*

He leaned over the rail, sunlight made him squint. Boot heels descended. He hugged the wall as a cracked, acoustically attuned voice sang:

"We'll meet again, don't know where, don't know when, But I know we'll meet again—"

Closing doors chopped off the song. It left Purdy weak, and thinking of his sadistic brute of a father who had deserved his filthy grave. The song lingered as adult logic contradicted childish thought.

Giddy, and using the stair rail, Jerry came slowly down, stark brightness creating illusion. God, he was hungry. Two days. If he could make it to The Copper Kettle and Edna Duffy, all starched apron and chintz tablecloths, he might relax, enjoy her special breakfast, have a laugh like old times.

He used an emergency exit off the main A & E. Avoiding two drivers having a crafty smoke, he used the ambulances as cover, pleased to breathe fresh air, feel the early breeze on his skin. The chill would burn off soon and he walked down sloping lawns, telling himself not to hurry, for hurrying might draw someone's attention, and he sure as hell wasn't going back in that room, no way.

Eventually, he emerged through a side gate and into the narrow streets of Tibb's Cove.

The Cove went back a few centuries, its history steeped in smuggling and revenue men, caves and wrecks, the off-shore tide race a trap to bathers, the deeper water beyond the point, a place to shun, at least that's what Jerry kept reminding himself.

Moon had seen to that. Didn't Jerry know what Moon's factory pumped into the sea? How Moon played with his computers? Enlisted the help of others? All sworn to secrecy they were, the workforce obliged to say nothing with a capital N. 'Fuck you, Moon. You'll get yours one day.'

Weakness pulled him onto a seat donated by some local. He looked down on Leggo town, its multicoloured roofs vying with one another, buildings crammed and stacked box-like into winding, cobbled streets which all led to the Promenade. The Prom, cluttered with closing down sales, fish and chip shops, sea food stalls, and the Air Museum.

'The museum. Ah!' Housed in a pre-Victorian four-storey block of granite, its paint-flaking exterior was about as inviting as the decayed exhibits Jerry had seen as a kid. He'd never been back.

One time there had been a notice of a guided tour to Hatcher's Field. **VISIT A REAL AIRFIELD** it had said. **TOURS TWICE DAILY 2/6d.**

Him and the others hadn't paid for that privilege. They had taken the easy way, the cheating way, the boys-doing-reckless-things way. Under the wire — after dark. FOOLS.

Forget it. 'I can't.'

The dunes looked sullen, a cloud diffusing the sun. The beach was empty. Silence was an intruder: houses, still asleep at this early hour, leaned into damp streets, no longer an artist's impression, sooty facades smacking of time-weariness.

Purdy skidded on a greasy chip wrapper, and kicked angrily at it. A butcher pulling down his blind to protect his fresh meat, eyed him warily.

'Morning,' the butcher said, 'lost a shoe I see.'

Purdy wasn't in the mood. 'Yeah,' he shot back, 'they only got the one yesterday. Gotta fetch the other in a week.'

'Sarky sod.' The butcher curled his lip. 'Best thing you can do is piss off back to where you came from. Your sort don't belong here.'

He wanted to say what's my sort, but let it go. He couldn't be bothered. His belly rumbled, his mind-picture of bacon, eggs and all the trimmings pulling him like filings to the magnet.

Cove hasn't changed, he told himself, just people. Nobody wants to know anymore. Look after number one, that's the law.

Progress hadn't sliced a hand across Tibb's Cove (except perhaps for Moon). Since pre-war days the landmarks had remained solid bastions, its lamp posts all cast Victorian, and the great clock, all scrolls and tails, above the archway leading to the shopping arcades, had stopped at three twenty three on a day no-one had been taking notice. Yet, Purdy knew, for all his lack of education, that The Cove smacked of a history as yet unwritten — a history seeded in 1943, perpetuated in 1954.

'Sweet Christ, will there ever be an end?'

The streets were as empty as the sky, weather eroded lime-stone cliffs guarding secrets best left untapped. Purdy limped down the street and underneath the fortune-teller's sign, totally unaware he was being watched.

CHAPTER 9

Nick Tyler had seen Purdy through the grimy window of his bedsit above Madame Zara's and turned away. Purdy was something Tyler didn't need, especially where Mattie Wells was concerned.

Tyler sneered at the room, annoyed he had been barracked here with the promise of something better soon. Hardly used to it, right now he couldn't figure a way out.

'Not enough room to swing a cat,' he said. Then again, he hadn't relished living with Mattie in the tumbledown heap of stone she had lovingly referred to as "my mother's place". Some things about it he had liked, others...? Well, they hadn't sat right in his scheme of things either. The damp walls and a nauseous smell of camphor had dulled what he liked to term his finely tuned senses. There had been that solitary book lying on its own on the shelf above the tiled fireplace. "Alice in Wonderland".

'I'm late,' he muttered, 'for a very important date.' And all it needs is a phone call. But why, suddenly, did he think about airfields?

'Nick, please come back to bed, and stop muttering to yourself.' Jane Lennard watched him through lidded eyes. She had awoken to find him gone, and was perturbed, especially after their re-discovery of each other. She held out a hand, which he grasped as he sat on the bed.

'What's bothering you?' Jane was concerned, but knew if she pushed too hard, she might risk him retreating into his shell again.

They had known each other some weeks, had really gotten to know one other after an especially wild night at HATTERS. That had been the first time she had let him, out there under the moon, amidst the dunes.

Nick gazed at a spot on the wall just above her head.

Jane didn't mind him not meeting her own gaze. Instead, she smiled coquettishly and flung back the covers. Her tanned skin beckoned.

Nick dissected the spot on the wall. He couldn't tell her he was thinking about Purdy, and Friday night, and Mattie, and how he felt about the cottage. He daren't. Or about the plane, or his computer expertise, and what Franklyn Moon demanded. Nick's past was subjugating people, Moon knew it, and had tapped into it. Women were a speciality, married, single, whoever. Most of them cared, but Nick cared very little for the niceties.

Jane tugged his arm. 'You're not listening. You don't really want me... do you?'

He didn't answer, thinking about a certain preacher who had been with Mattie. Man of God? In a pig's eye.

Jane's hands slowly slid down his torso. He grabbed her so suddenly she yelled and pulled away. He held her wrists, dark eyes searching her face, and Jane realised the whispered endearments, the yells as they had climaxed simultaneously had been replaced by a nothingness that spoke of ill-use. Nice knowing you again, but this time the party really is over.

She felt vulnerable, and sought refuge in the bed-clothes. 'That's it, goodbye fun time. And to think you almost married

Mattie Wells.' Jane's eyes were like flint. 'What happened, Nicky, too much of a woman for you was she?' She straight-away thought how cruel it sounded, but it was too late.

She studied him as he shrugged into his dressing gown, and wondered whether to shoot another barb. She did: 'I'd be better off with Gavin,' then wondered why, because it wasn't true.

Nick set the kettle to boil on the two-ring calor gas burner.

'Did you hear me?' Jane struggled to pull on her panties beneath the clothes. Only when she had tugged her green jumper on inside out, not that it mattered, did she throw back the quilt and shrug into her jeans.

'Coffee or tea?' Nick sounded too casual, seagull cries and the kettle's shrill whistle heightening the tension.

She fluffed her dark, wavy hair in a resigned gesture. 'I won't hold you to anything, Nick.' As if she could.

She sat at a tiny table and cleared last night's foil containers to one side, ignoring the dried sweet and sour stains on the scratched formica. Stirring away her frustrations she sipped her coffee. 'It's been great. We enjoyed each other—' Brave face, gal, she kept telling herself. Don't let him see it bothers you.

'Say again.' He sat opposite, a foil carton falling to the floor. A fork rattled.

'You don't listen, Nick.' Jane was upset. That it had come to this really rattled her. All the sweet talk, the lies. Sure I'll marry you, he'd said, and persuaded her into doing it without a condom. Jesus, what was I thinking?

'What is it really? Mattie Wells still in there somewhere?' His scowl didn't faze her. 'A lump of cold marble, that's you, Nick. Everything great as long as Nicky's enjoying it, right? Everybody else can go... Oh, what's the point?'

'You said it.' The blank stare again, as though he was else-where and didn't give a toss anyway.

Jane stood, her knee jarring the table, coffee spilled, dripped to the floor, pattering on the foil carton like a rapid heartbeat. She shied away from his reaching fingers. 'Don't... just don't.' She decided she was seeing him for what he really was — Do I really know? — and hammered home the point. 'You're a dropout, Nick. You came here from wherever, and you're going nowhere.'

She hoped it would hurt, but she was rewarded with the same, iron melting stare. 'Just what is this town doing to us, to you, me, everybody? It's like being trapped in a vacuum.'

'What do you mean?' Nick swilled the cups in the sink.

'My, my, you actually spoke.' Her sarcasm dripped like venom. 'You actually said something. There is life in there.' She jerked him round to face her. 'We had a plane shooting up the beach, Nick, killing people. I mean actually blowing them to bits. Doesn't that mean anything to you?'

His shrug said it all. He turned on the shower in the small cubicle to the right of the sink, threw off his robe and stepped in. The curtain swishing closed was the final insult.

The gush of water hid her exit.

The breeze scoured away the residue of the confrontation, yet Jane still felt unclean. She walked along the shoreline playing the game of dodging the tide as it obliterated her footprints.

She looked behind her. 'Just as if I'd never been.' She ached inside.

Maybe she should leave Tibb's Cove, start again. Her parents didn't care, always out at this party or the other, playing up to Moon and his cronies. Even the drama crowd were becoming a bore. 'Time to change before it's too late.'

The cliff wouldn't be ignored: it loomed solid and terrifying, the memory of Gavin shielding, protecting and then suddenly gone as though he hadn't even been there, a little perplexing.

'Cowards and fools,' she shouted. There was no-one to hear, and in itself, that was strange.

Climbing over the breakwater, she bypassed Macey's Nose, and the dark, unwelcome cave at its foot. Sun sparkled on the water, surf tumbled over the splayed hand of rocks where the beach sloped upwards to O'Connell's cottage.

Jane sat on the damp sand, thoughts overlapping like the waves. What had she said to Nick? *All caught in a vacuum.* 'We are. We dance to a tune laid down by time.' And perhaps Franklyn Moon, her conscience reminded. The mighty Moon, Lord of the Manor of Tibb's Cove, Lord of all he surveys. 'Or thinks he is.'

Jane nibbled her lip, fiddled with the strap of her bag. 'It's like they're all being held here against their will.'

So, what makes you any different? Her conscience pricked again.

She shivered, the breeze cantered up the beach, dust devils digging their forks into her exposed skin. O'Connell's cottage door shrieked on old hinges, Jane moving towards it. A sudden quiet yielded the plaintive crying of —

'A dog?' She drew nearer an upturned boat and on all fours, leaned in to investigate.

A cold black nose nuzzling her hand made her jump. Then a pink tongue gave it a cursory lick.

O'Leary had been hiding for too long. With his master gone, he had remained in the only place familiar to him.

'Here, boy,' Jane coaxed, happy that she could at least please someone. 'Come on, it's okay, I won't bite.' She giggled. 'And you won't bite me, oh no you won't.'

The dog eased out and shook loose sand from his ebony coat, brown, sad eyes seeking hers. He sat and offered a paw.

Jane took it. 'Very pleased to meet you.'

The cottage door slammed, O'Leary's low growl hardly

disguising the threat.

'Easy, boy, easy, it's only the wind.' She hooked fingers in his collar, and together they went up the rickety steps to pause before the door.

Admittedly Jane wasn't too happy about the location's sheltered aspects. Rimmed with high cliffs, it confirmed how alone, and vulnerable she felt.

'Is anyone there?' she called, disturbed by the echo bouncing off the cliff.

She pushed the door: the place smelled empty.

A stained mug and a plate of dried crusts sat on a table. Beside them a glass and a half bottle of Jamiesons, and a foil package of thick twist next to a briar pipe.

'Definitely empty.' She ran her fingers through the dust on an oak dresser which held a full Willow Pattern dinner service, four of the plates sporting hairline cracks.

'What the — ?' She struggled and backed off, trying to free her hair from a tangle of nets festooning the ceiling, glass weights reflected the light through the open door. She kicked a gaggle of lobster pots in the corner, O'Leary barking, darting away as they tumbled.

'Well, Dog,' she said, 'we'll have to watch our step.' She leaned against the newel post of an uncarpeted staircase leading upwards into dull, matt shades of an upper floor.

Jane scrutinized a framed commendation hanging to the left of a scullery door, and read: '"For bravery in the face of the enemy. Awarded to Arthur O'Connell, Navigator, 29th/30th December, 1943... raid on Berlin". Mmm, looks like your master's a veteran, Dog.'

She nodded approvingly at the DFC hanging from a rusty tack beside the commendation.

The scullery was a dismal place, lit — when she found the switch — by a filthy bulb. The room reeked of stale leftovers, and unwashed pots. O'Leary nudged her, and tendered a muffled bark.

'Hungry, right?'

His tail answered.

'Thought so.' Jane rummaged and discovered a half full can of dog food which she spooned onto the cleanest plate available and laughed as he shovelled it around the floor.

In the main room, Jane amused herself looking at photographs splayed across a battered, green baize-less card table. On the oak mantle over the inglenook fireplace she noticed a sheathed bayonet. 'Thought airmen didn't have bayonets.' She glanced about her again. 'By the look of this lot I'll bet Mr. O'Connell's a collector of sorts.'

There were more pictures shoved behind a pewter mug. Smiling airmen beneath the belly of a large plane with — and she grinned — a Grumpy motif painted on the nose, Disney's cartoon character complete with floppy hat, arms folded and a miserable expression bordering on malevolence. Another had bombing up crew, a control tower; there were shots of a guard-house and aircrew lolling in chairs outside and inside Nissen huts whose potbellied stoves smelled of warmth and coffee constantly on the boil. Distant humour, the rattle of dice on a board game, the chink of glasses, rattle of dominoes, the soft shuffle of cards.

Seven men smiled from another picture, the one in the centre looking straight into the lens, a half smile on his not unhand-some face. His hat was worn at a rakish angle synonymous with aircrew. The other six were a mixture of long, short, tubby and balding, one very like the man they called Tom who ran the seafood stall by the pier. The seven dwarfs, thought Jane wryly.

On the back were faded autographs which she read aloud: 'Arthur O'Connell — Tall, dark, wavy hair. So that's what you looked like. Tom Sheridan. Yes, the seafood man. George Purdy. Purdy? He's fat. Wonder if he's related to Mattie's uncle? So the one in the centre has to be Melville Cross—' It was a guess, but somehow the name fitted.

O'Leary, finished eating and growled from the scullery doorway, hackles up.

'What is it, Dog?' Jane turned, squinting against the glare, at the shape there backlit by the sun.

Stepping forward, completely oblivious to O'Leary's warning, she said, 'I'm sorry, I know it's rude of me, but the door was open, and your dog was hungry so I—'

Odd, she was thinking. Why doesn't he say something? She stepped back, butting the card table. The air felt heavy, unbreathable. Instinct, coupled with a blind sense for self preservation, and her earlier thought of how vulnerable she had made herself in this quiet place, forced her to grab the bayonet.

Still he didn't move, then: 'Hi, Jane Lennard, name's Mel Cross—' The drawl grated. '—aaalll the way from Sweetwater, Texas. I jest know we'll git along.' The picture image smiled that same laid back smile.

O'Leary bared his teeth, the threat ignored by the intruder.

The bayonet shook in her hand as Jane thrust it before her. 'Don't... don't come any closer.' The tremor in her voice betrayed her anxiety.

Cross held out his arms in a throwaway gesture. 'I on'y wanna git acquainted, honey.'

'How come you know my name.'

His smile, the echo of a voice which seemed to emanate from behind his unmoving lips, reminded Jane of a dummy jiggled by wires. She asked again, voice hardly audible.

He took one pace, Jane moved backwards, the table juddering on the stone flagged floor.

'Cove's a small place, hon. Come to know many in my travels... Like your Mum.'

Jane hated the innuendo, yet what he'd said stirred something. Another picture on her Mum's bureau at home.

A further step.

'That's enough. No nearer.' Jane felt trapped: she had nowhere to run.

His laugh curled and stayed. It was the same non-sound she had experienced on the cliffs with Gavin, that stirring of air. And it was apparent again. Jane could *feel* it. Above the cottage... behind clouds which had surreptitiously darkened the day.

Cross said, 'Someone to watch over me, darlin'.' His eyes flicked skywards.

By the scullery door, Jane trod on the dog food tin which O'Leary, after licking the plate clean, had collected from the drainer where she had left it, and promptly done it service. The can scooted, taking her, momentarily, off balance.

Cross came at her, Jane tightening her grip on the bayonet, even as O'Leary shot around her to leap straight at him. He hovered, Jane bringing up the bayonet in one gut-tearing stroke.

The dog, bewildered, fell on his belly, unsure why he had met little resistance.

Jane screamed out, as Cross, his asinine grin still mocking, watched the bayonet clatter to the floor — the bayonet which, like the dog, had passed straight through him.

CHAPTER 10

It certainly wasn't a fun house joke.

'WHAT IN HELL ARE YOU?' Jane screeched, courage lying on the floor with the bayonet. 'TELL ME... tell me.' It trailed off, fear's icy knot tightening.

O'Leary was hiding beneath the boat again: the air whistled like a blacksmith's bellows, it stank of decomposition. Of bad things.

Jane slammed into the table, photographs swirling up and around her. Mel Cross stayed put, the grey wash of light from outside creating an illusion of transparency, his flesh, indeed the bones beneath, like cheap plastic.

Jane wanted Nick, Gavin, the whole damned populace of Tibb's Cove. 'Somebody... pleeeaasse.'

Sidestepping, she ran up the stairs, dust motes floating, choking. On the tiny landing she kicked a lath door, the bath-room beyond tacky with the aromas of Old Spice and damp towels. It offered nothing, its one window far too small an exit.

The bedroom was her final hope. The unmade bed was grimy, a leaning wardrobe devoid of its doors, spilled clothes, a marble washstand held a residue of brackish water, and a curled HOME SWEET HOME embroidery had been nailed to the flaking plaster wall. The curtains were still drawn against the light. Thick twist permeated the air, caught in O'Connell's clothes, his Aran sweater thrown over the brass bed. Neglect and hopelessness smacked Jane between the eyes. Destroyed cobwebs floated to the floor: Jane yanked the curtains open, spiders scurrying into wall cracks.

The cottage began to vibrate. Hardly noticeable at first, Jane felt the floorboards tremble. An ornament toppled, rolled off the windowsill to shatter on the floor; clothes slid off precarious hangers and behind her the door creaked.

Gripping the window catch, she jerked it upwards and pushed outwards. It worked, the window didn't.

A rusted casement, glued with paint and time, and bitumen black mould; old metal grinding as Jane willed it to open… pushing… pushing…

In The Copper Kettle, Purdy drained his third mug of tea, his jowls glistened with bacon fat, egg yoke congealed on his shirt front. A belch rumbled. 'Right nice, Edna, I needed that.'

Edna Duffy's rotund, ruddy face was serious as she spooned baked beans onto three rounds of toast. 'No good'll come of this, Jerry, you mark my words.' She turned off the poached eggs and slid them onto the beans. She gestured with a spoon. 'Don't forget, I was one of your crowd in the old days. Cinema, dancing, canoodling on the playing fields. I know what you an' Dykes got up to.'

She turned on a smile she hardly felt. 'Here you are, sir, sorry for the delay. One pound fifty eight please.'

A bus driver, the only other customer, sorted out change. Edna waiting patiently as it was tipped into her palm.

'Tips, eh? Still, I can do with the coins.' Edna fed them into the till and shut the drawer.

'Fetch a cuppa over, Edna.' Jerry pushed the chair opposite with his foot. 'Sit a while before the rush starts.'

Edna laughed, a real earthy sound. 'Rush? Bless you, lovey, them days are long away. No more seasons left. Wind blows cold off the sea, an' me bones ache. No, no more, it's time t'go, lad.' She stared off into space for a second or so. 'Something about The Cove lately, kinda gives me a prickly feeling.'

'Yeah,' Jerry said quietly, 'I felt it not two nights ago.'

'One time this place would hum. Me an' Phyllis'd be cooking and serving for all we was worth. Now she's gone.'

'Me an' Dykes used t'plague her something chronic. Hey, recall that plastic fried egg Dykes substituted and then complained? You never let on either. Gave 'er a tellin' off remember?'

'Don't kid yourself, Jerry.' Edna blew on her tea and sipped it. 'If memory serves, Phyllis handed them hot sweets around to you lot a week or so later. They made your gums giggle. Sold plenty of cold drinks that day I did.'

They laughed, the humour just another tack in time, Edna wearing a faraway smile, oblivious to the party of schoolkids walking past, or the sound of car horns. Or someone singing.

Purdy heard the singing.

The driver shovelled beans into his mouth, and immersed himself in his newspaper.

'*...meet again some sunny day...*'

The copper kettle on the hob in the corner — the very one Edna had placed there on the day she took possession — rattled very slightly.

'That's funny.' Edna stood, frowning when her china cup rattled in its saucer. 'Now that is a mite strange.'

Jerry pulled her back into the chair, his meal threatening. 'Edna, it's nothin'.'

'Nothing? I'll lay bets it's that Franklyn Moon and his factory, aye and his computer fiddling, on the Old Beach Road. Told you, nothing good'll come of it. Bastard during the war was Moon. Thought he owned everything and everybody then.' She looked formidable, hands on hips, great bosom heaving. Jabbing a finger at Jerry she said: 'Told you he was no good when you and Dykes palled about with him. Pollution is all he chucks out. Small wonder Cove's not fit for fish or man. Petitions one after another an' what good did it do? Too many friends up the top has our Mister Moon. None of us sees 'im, locked away in his big 'ouse, or riding around in that big car with the blacked out windows—'

'Tinted, Edna,' Jerry corrected. '*Tinted* windows.'

'Aye, them, but y'still can't see the sod.'

'I don't see him either,' Jerry said, 'and I work...'

The drone was deafening.

Even the driver, a portion of egg halfway to his mouth, paused and peered through the lace curtains gracing Edna's Georgian Bow window.

Purdy had to hide like he would when Emmy frightened him, or when George tormented, the young Purdy feeling nothing but loathing for the man he had once called Dad.

Every pot rattled, a jug toppled from a delft rail and smashed; the driver dropped his fork and beans and gawped through the window again. 'Bleedin' hell, look at that.'

Purdy didn't need to, he knew what was coming. And he knew it was searching for him, all because of what he had done. In 1954. It wanted rid of 'em all so it could come back proper-like. First Dykes, now him. Then it'd be Len. Jesus God, when would it stop?

Edna, curious, shrugged off Jerry's hand.

The clouds had parted, blasted apart in a massive burst of displaced air. Kids yelled, applauded, four teenagers cheered, everyone on that promenade gazing skywards.

Edna marched to the door and opened it. 'What is going on?'

Jerry slid to the floor, a mind-picture of Dykes's dance of

death obliterating all else. He sought sanctuary behind the heavy wooden counter as blood pounded his eye sockets.

Hazy sunlight lit the prom, troubling the eyes of some one hundred or so onlookers, at least twenty of them in an open topped day trippers' bus. Disbelief moulded itself as they saw the huge plane steering a straight course some thirty feet above lamp post height.

From his window above Madame Zara's, Tyler saw it and thought of Jane, what he had said. And what he had to do.

On the funfair, by the pier, Gavin Pountney paused in laying out the air rifles on the target range. He dived behind the flimsy hardboard stall. He too, thought about Jane Lennard.

Gavin felt unreal, like he had the other night. The plane had banked, and it felt as though he had been sucked up in the vortex created by the displaced air, almost as though he had become a part of... 'Scary. Jesus!'

'Is it a fly past?' queried a retired, tweed coated man of his wife. 'Bit like that Dam Busters thing in Derby—'

Three ricochets tore out his words, blood and an extra hot mint spewed onto the pavement, his body laid on the air before falling backwards into a wife who had no face.

Panic threw people into each other, torn bodies tumbled to the road. Tarmac was gouged, the open topped bus laid waste like a can of sardines smothered in ketchup. The driver's cap and half his head landed on the lap of a man trying to push his small daughter under a seat. Six schoolboys danced, their spasms taking them into the road to tumble into the gutter as the plane's aft gun turret spun through forty-five degrees.

The Copper Kettle's window caved in, flying glass shredding the driver's face. He choked, his coffee tipped, pooled, mixed with arterial blood jetting from his neck.

Edna raved, even when bullets tore open her shoulder and slammed her into the counter, her head cracking the display of pastries so lovingly baked that morning.

Purdy would not come out, his childhood filled with gnomes, and a groping, gloved hand reaching from beneath his bed.

'I... I didn't mean to, Mam. Me an' Dykes didn't mean to. An' Mattie... she oughtn't to have gone to the church fete that day. I told her not to. The airman belonged to Emmy, an' Emmy tol' me not to. Said not t'mess with things.'

He sobbed, his breathless diatribe out of context, intermingled with prayers and pleas.

Exactly as Jane Lennard was praying at the same time.

She heard the firing in the distance, and could see smoke billowing, and still the window wouldn't budge.

The hand grabbed her by the hair, and flung her across the sweat and Old Spice stinking bed.

Jane closed her eyes, but fought the hands tearing at her clothes, kneading her breasts. She kicked, and punched, her overwhelming sense of dread compounded by the fact... *that it was all in her head.*

There was no-one there, only empty air and yet... hands caressed, fingers probed.

She gripped the bedstead, the brass as cold as that which covered her. Her screams climbed as her legs were wrenched apart.

'DEAR SWEET JESUS... NOOOOOO!'

This was the vacuum, and she was immersed in it, unable to breathe, her cries for salvation falling on the ears of a church which had been so foully tainted all those years ago. The grave smell was overpowering, that coupled with the foetid stench of seawater, and she gagged.

From the landing she could hear the frantic barking as O'Leary pounded into the room to dive at the threshing heap of bedding. The sheets spiralled, the dog snapping, even as

Jane fell off the bed to jar her elbows on the boards.

Rolling towards the wall, she pulled at her torn clothes, mesmerised by the dog attacking what was only a heap of bedding last used by his late, unlamented master.

She screamed out, and grabbed the dog, O'Leary snapping at her in his fury, Jane crying out: 'IT'S ME, DOG. ME!' Then she flung everything, even the mattress off the bed, one sheet still suspended in the air like an angry ghost, some *thing* beneath it.

O'Leary grabbed a corner of the sheet and pulled, Jane sickened at the amorphous shape beneath. Here was flesh, yet not flesh, the skeleton beneath visible, tiny burning pinpricks of light in rotted sockets, a bony hand in a cracked leather glove groping for the dog.

Jane gripped O'Leary's collar and pulled, and thankfully, they both tumbled onto the landing as the bed shot sideways. A hideous moan filled the room, the very window Jane had been unable to open, blasted to bits.

In the sudden quiet, a whisper: 'I have returned for my soul.'

In its aftermath, the silence was overpowering.

Jane and the dog ran onto the shingle: the sea chuckled, it mocked, Jane on her knees drinking frantic gulps of fresh air. She sobbed her anguish, her fear into the dog, as O'Leary licked her tears. Sick to her very core, she inspected the bruises and knew all of it had been real. She dare not look back.

Running, muscles crying for release from the merciless demands she was putting on them, Jane still shrieked her fear into an unconcerned day. Tears still clouded her vision as she drove herself, every yard a reward. Seaweed and driftwood were obstacles, the ominous pall of smoke hanging over The Cove another positive threat.

Every pumping step, every heartbeat became a thought:

ordinary life, education the same; parents had treated her okay... 'Grown up now, Janey,' her dad had said, 'make your own life.' As much as they cared? And Nick? What about Nick? Well, Nick didn't give a fart in hell.

Slower now, breathing hard won, Jane realised her parents hadn't just ignored her, they had rejected her. Where were their loving arms, her dad's whispered endearments? What had happened to her mother's guidance? The teaching her to cook and sew and all things women do? 'I wanted all that,' she sobbed and found fresh solace in the dog — the only *real* living being which meant something.

'Mum and Dad have each other. I... I have... nothing!'

She stamped a foot in anger, staring at the imprint in wet sand, the sea reshaping it. In desperation, and a real effort to come to terms with everything she said: 'Get real, Janey. This is stupid. Things like this don't happen in Tibb's Cove.'

Can you believe that? If so, you haven't heard the one about the girl raped in the church. Or the teenagers who trespassed on Hatcher's Field.

Voices. In her head. Ignore them. Weak, and with the break-water hiding her from the cottage, she screwed her eyes against the glare off the water, scanning it, seeing and hearing only seabirds.

Just an ordinary day, she told herself, but still insecurity forced her to ask herself why she felt so alone. 'Who can I turn to?'

The dog nuzzled her. 'Oh sure, I've got you.'

Stomach cramps forced her to lean over and heave. She knew it couldn't be over. Whatever it was back there wouldn't leave it at that.

She panicked when the elongated shadow engulfed her.

CHAPTER 11

Purdy realised how pathetic he must look as he held out his plastered arm towards the girl. 'Help me. Please.'

He hoped he was doing the right thing. She might run, or worse set the dog on him. He disliked dogs and edged away.

Jane studied him. 'I know you, don't I? I saw you on Friday night after the — You were standing in the middle of the road before the ambulance left.' Lord, he looks pitiful in those shabby clothes. Jane hid a grin as she caught a glimpse of one big toe peeping from the shredded sock on his shoeless foot.

Not that I'm much better, she told herself. Her jeans were torn, T shirt ripped from neck to armpit, and she knew he could see the bruises.

'I... I don't... I won't hurt you,' Purdy said, his breath coming in short bursts. His smile was throwaway. 'Not very good at running. Had to get away... back there. It... I mean it was like hell. Worse.' He dropped to his knees. 'It came back... people are dead... An' I don't know why. I DON'T KNOW WHY.'

O'Leary growled. 'Easy boy.' Jane grabbed his collar.

Jerry struggled to his feet. 'To hell with you, you're all the same.' He stumbled to the breakwater and stared out to sea, aware the girl was beside him.

'Maybe you aren't like the rest,' he mumbled. 'Trouble is I get so confused. Y'see I drink a lot 'cos I'm not, well, sort of like most folks if you know what I mean. I'm fat and ugly, an' I —'

She was listening to him, and he felt heartened by the fact that she didn't treat him like a leper.

'I used to come here a lot when I was younger,' he jabbered. 'I'd sit in the dunes and read my paper, and sup beer with Dykes. Dykes is my best mate, on'y one I got. Go back aways me an' Dykes. His wife's nice. You'd like Jaqui. They live out by the park in one of those pre-war semis.'

Jane let him ramble, it was obviously doing him good. And the more he talked, the more relaxed she became. And she found herself involved in what he was saying.

He talked about Mattie. 'Wedding was fated from the start. I knew she wouldn't marry Tyler. Little turd. God's gift an' all that.'

Jane silently agreed.

'I was in The Copper Kettle,' Purdy said. 'Edna… salt of the earth she is, she got shot. I sent for the ambulance but I guess somebody'd already done it. I like t'do what I can for folk, for friends. Didn't stay 'cos I was scared they'd come back for me. Don't like hospitals.'

'Who might come back? I mean why did you think that, Mr… er? I'm sorry.'

'Jerry Purdy,' he responded smiling. 'You can call me Jerry if you like. The ambulance. I meant the ambulance.'

'Oh. Oh yes. And it's Jerry. Right. I'm Jane Lennard. My parents have that huge bungalow up near the Imperial Hotel at the top.'

Why did I tell him that? Pretentious. Why should he care?

'Nice up there. I'd like to live in a big place, have a nice car, money. Emily wouldn't let me.'

'Who's Emily?'

He watched a crab scuttle into a deep pool. Wish I could run away. Hide until it was all done.

Jane prompted: 'Who is Emily, Jerry? And why did you run?'

'Run?' He looked vacant and pondered the question.

Jane waited, pulling her coat about her, a chill breeze uncomfortable. O'Leary sank to his belly, head on his paws, yet very alert.

'I guess,' Jerry eventually said, 'I've been doing that all my life. Always the odd one out, that's me. Dad hated me. Mam was great. But I never did have any luck with girls. I mean look at me, I'm like a beached whale. Who'd want me?'

'They say everyone has a purpose in life, Jerry. Sometimes I wonder what mine is.'

'You? Aw, come on, you're nice looking.' He frowned as he studied her. 'You've hurt yourself. Those bruises. And the scratches...'

She told him. Everything. Feeling that if she didn't she would flip entirely. And in the telling Jane detected Jerry's sudden fear when she mentioned Cross. She laughed at his apologetic, embarrassed manner when she told him about Tyler.

'But Cross. I mean how can something hurt me when it isn't really there, Jerry?' She began to tremble, Jerry touching her arm, a simple, yet to Jane, welcome gesture.

'Please, don't, it'll be okay.' But Jerry didn't really believe that.

Jane pulled away, suddenly unsure of his intentions. Or was it the memory of what had happened? Surely, this man wouldn't... No, it wasn't in him. Not Jerry Purdy. He was a lost soul. They were both lost souls.

'Your telling me this, Jane, is just like Emily would tell 'em. She scared me did Emmy.' He studied the white caps chasing landward. 'Emmy was the worst kind o' woman any man could have as kin. You can't ever know what she did.'

Jane touched his injured arm. 'I don't, but I would like to.'

His head came up from where he had been studying her artistic fingers tracing patterns on the plaster. Even with sand in their nails, those fingers looked lovely. 'Do you really mean it, Jane? You want me to tell it?'

She nodded. 'Can we sit? I feel a little wobbly.'

The sun had warmed again, cloud shadows retreating. They leaned against the breakwater, the dog's head across Jane's thighs.

'Cross—' said Purdy, '—was in the church the day of the fete. A name in a book is all he was, but he was there, Jane, just as you saw him at O'Connell's place. He went missing, that is three Lancaster bombers went missing on a night raid over Berlin.' He paused. 'You sure you want to know?'

'I guess I'll regret it, but yes I do.'

The pools rippled, distant smoke grew sparse, and Jerry went on: 'Everybody thought it was Reverend Black did that to Mattie, but I know different. Third Sunday in June it was. Best hats and new suits, get the drift? Len, my brother-in-law, looked real good. He's Mattie's dad. Proud wasn't in it. There was Mattie all dressed in white with little bows and things on her dress. She loved fairs and things. I treated her to a few roundabout rides and such, and I recall she won about a pound on the roller penny.' He grinned. 'Yeah, lucky she was before… Anyway folks looked real nice, and Mattie had a rose entwined in her dark hair. I like dark hair. Hair like Mattie's, like yours. Like dark hair, I do.

'I was twenty-six then, an' not quite as big as I am now. Me an' Dykes got really pissed. Oh, sorry…'

'No problem. Please go on.'

'Right. Well the beer an' whisky chasers did it. Mam had me

go on a diet so I could get in my one and only suit, but I couldn't fasten the waistcoat. Still, with the jacket fastened nobody noticed. Doubt whether they'd've cared anyway.

'I was inspecting gravestones. Not that I could read what was writ, but it made me look sober. Then Emily whispered in my ear... I mean I hadn't heard her come over. She was just there, an' she said: "All this God thing and raising funds for the church is garbage, Jeremiah, but it keeps Len happy, so I don't argue."

'Her pinched face — she had piercing, cold blue eyes did Emily, eyes which scorched your soul. What Len saw in her I can't guess. She always bothered me, even when I was a kid. Mam always said she was different. "A heathen" Mam called her.

'"*Sometimes things return*", Emmy told me, and all the bad tales she used to tell came worming back. I still have nightmares. I mean, I was twenty-six—' he allowed himself a sour grin. 'I couldn't let her believe I was still scared at that age.'

'So, what happened?' Jane prompted.

'I went into the church lookin' for Mattie. Somebody, I forget who, told me she'd spilled a drink down her dress and that Black had taken her to get it cleaned up. Didn't like Black, gave me the creeps, he did. Thoughts of him alone with Mattie sort of made me want to go and find her, if y'see what I mean.

'Christ, he was a smarmy so-an'-so was Black. Oh, he always looked smart with his slicked black hair and nice pressed suit but that collar he wore seemed out of place on him. He looked a lot like my dad did Black. I recall the choir was practising hymns, an' all the crap. It was hot, so the main doors were open. Churches are mostly cold even when it's warm, but on that day it was bloody hot. I even undid my jacket and my tie. Didn't matter about the waist-coat 'cos half the other blokes had done the same.

'I still see Emily smirking at me after I'd asked where Black was, almost like she knew something I didn't.

'She told me again about the pop being spilled down Mattie's dress. Mattie was going on five so yeah, I was bothered. I mean Black's reputation, rumour and all, it put the wind up me a bit. I looked for Len but couldn't see him, an' there was Emily smiling like the friggin' Queen in Snow White.

'The sun got hotter, brighter as I went into the church, and I could see Mel Cross, standing to attention by the RAF flag. Emily had followed me, and it scared me when she called out Cross's name. Then Black peered around the vestry door like Dracula with his widow's peak an' all. The choir was singing, other folk were looking around the church, some doing them brass rubbings and such, others taking pictures. And it was so bloody hot. God, it was like a football crowd all of a sudden, they all went loopy. I could hear... sounds. I could smell burning fuel, and I saw Cross follow Black's beckoning finger. Bastard went through the vestry door.'

Jane momentarily closed her eyes, pictures of the church, the beach cottage, the night on the cliff, her time with Nick, hurriedly scrolled down her mind.

'Want me to stop?' Jerry asked, feeling he may have over-stepped himself. 'You gone a bit pale.'

It's a paradox, Jane was thinking. Indeed, maybe they both were. The question: Where do I go from here? seemed hardly worth answering.

In fact, they did both realise where they were going at the same time and Jane voiced it for them both. 'We have to go on together. What's past is memory. We must stop whatever is threatening us, and Tibb's Cove, right?'

Jerry agreed, sure that at least he realised what she meant. He was content to ride with it, reasoning that with Jane as an ally, the force, their joint force, might help.

'In the vestry,' Jerry said, 'Black had taken off Mattie's dress. Mattie was crying as she watched Emily lay herself on the vestry table. I couldn't stop it. There was some... some power preventing me doing a thing. I recall the white cloth under Emily, and round stains where cups had been placed on it.

'Cross was a Yank, but you know that. Flight Lieutenant he was, and he fiddled with a key ring as he unbuttoned his flies. Black was unbuttoning his own at the same time, like... like they were doing exactly that because it was expected, movements, gestures all the same. And the smell in that room was like an open coffin.'

Jerry was red in the face now, his anger scouring his heavy, tired features. 'Cross flung Emily's skirts up and took her, an' I wanted to stop it, all the while wondering what Cross had against me an' mine. Wondering why he'd come back... and how.'

Come back for my soul echoed in Jane's head, but again she kept it to herself.

'I was part of it, Jane. Jus' like you at O'Connell's place. Has to be connections. And there was Mattie watching her Mam doing it... even as Black was shoving himself at her.

'I wasn't seeing Black anymore. The grinning face was my dad's face, but I knew it couldn't have been... kept telling myself it wasn't, willing him to go back, just like I was willing Cross to go back. Somebody, Len I think, hammered on the door, but Em was screaming out: 'MEL. MEL.' And then she stared at Mattie and wearing that horrible grin she always wore, she said: 'Mattie, meet your real father.'

'Black thrust himself at Mattie, Mattie screeching and yelling enough to raise the roof, her collapsing... CHRIST, it was... God, I don't know. I just don't know.'

Jane felt sick, at a loss. She knew what had happened to her at the cottage and realised what it must have been like for a child of four? She buried her face in the dog's fur.

Jerry couldn't stop now: he was incensed, aching to relive that awful chapter, to spit it out, have done with it. 'I grabbed Mattie and hit Black, all the time knowing I was punching the thing I hated most. Emily still laughed, she screeched, as I opened the door and shoved Mattie into Len's arms.

'I know my father couldn't have been there, yet...'

'You mean it's impossible because photographs don't come to life,' Jane said in an abstract way.

Purdy searched the azure sky, its colour, its brightness contradicting. 'The bombers are up there, Jane, and with 'em is the fear. All because I meddled. ME.'

Jane gripped his hand. 'It isn't over then?'

Jerry shook his head. 'Cross said something to me that day. He said: *"You have something I want."* And that really scared me shitless. It was his look, the way his gloved finger stabbed at me.' Purdy appealed for comfort from Jane and was disappointed she had none to give.

O'Leary's shrill bark of impatience broke the awful tension.

'Okay, Dog,' Jane said in an effort to maintain a little light-heartedness, 'I guess you're hungry again.'

Nicky, she called inside herself, why couldn't you be different?

Purdy sketched the outline of an aeroplane in the sand. 'It was Franklyn Moon who talked us into going to Hatcher's Field y'know.' He glanced at Jane. 'Nobody ever sees Moon. He sits in his office, or at home, or rides in a car with tinted windows and he plays with computers, has done for years. Half his damn factory is automated. Skeleton staff is all, me amongst 'em, just to keep an eye on things, do the sweeping up. But we don't ever go to the big office, the one that's all air conditioned, where screens are on all the time. Or his house up by the Field. My guess is he's watching us, come to that he oversees the whole town. It's like we're living our lives through him.' It petered out. 'I'm rambling aren't I?'

Jane picked up on that, and said quietly, 'It's like looking through a glass darkly.'

He'd heard it somewhere and thought how apt it was. Jane eased herself up, her face distorted slightly by pain. 'Moon could well turn out to be the benefactor of Tibb's Cove, Jerry, but I think we've talked enough. I'm cold, tired and hungry, not necessarily in that order. Can we leave, please?'

Purdy blinked up at her. 'Sure we can. And thanks for listening, Jane.' He allowed her to help him up, not that it was easy. 'Bit of a weight aren't I?'

Jane tried to laugh and said, 'I had a horse once, a heavy old thing it was, but we were friends just the same.'

'I like you.' Purdy managed a smile despite his dark thoughts.

'You're not so bad yourself. Now come on, let's go home and I'll autograph that arm for you.'

'You're the first to offer.'

'Well, you know what they say, to make friends you need to have something in common. I guess we have.'

CHAPTER 12

Gavin Pountney eventually emerged from behind the flimsy barricade of the shooting stall thinking: Tibb's Cove used to be fun. The clown's high pitched laugh at the entrance to the Fun House attested to it.

His life had been an upward struggle, largely due to others. Twenty-one's a great age if you got money, friends and a likeable personality, those attributes sadly lacking in Gavin. Right this minute he wished he had listened to his parents way back when he might have fitted into a niche far removed from that of fairground barker. Attitude didn't help. People ignored him, not least Jane Lennard. There had been amphetamine experiments. Him and Freddie, a co-barker, and about the only individual who tolerated him, maybe because they had drugs as a compadre. Freddie had coerced him into taking LSD. 'Do y'good, mate. Take you out of yerself.'

It hadn't helped Georgie on the Dodgems, the one with the buck-toothed girlfriend. Riding high on drugs, Gavin had argued about change, and ended up breaking the lad's jaw, and cracking three ribs with his steel toe-capped boots. He had nearly waved bye-bye to his job over that.

The clown laughed, and for once, Gavin agreed. Didn't it just emphasise his lack of experience, his ignorance? Having started out in the false belief that the world owed him, Gavin realised maybe it was him who owed the world — or rather this small, dark corner of it: The Cove.

That business on the cliff the other night had made him feel real vulnerable. The worst part, he wasn't too sure why. That he hadn't belonged here, or anywhere as far as it went, was an understatement. But that other brain-bashing thought, that he wasn't a part of his own body, the one he was real familiar with, was unsettling, and a tad scary. He put it down to drugs, and prayed it was just that. And he could rectify it, he could stop taking 'em.

Dusting cobwebs and dust from his black cords, Gavin swore when he noticed the scratch on his left Doc and tried to rub it off with spit. Forty-five quid off a lorry they'd cost, enough to part with on his pittance.

This time he didn't respond to the clown's laughing. 'Fuck you, red nose,' he retorted, thinking how great it would feel to smash the perspex dome surrounding it and ring its cackling neck. He stopped the action. After all, here was more down-the-road territory, and despite everything he needed the money, and the status of being in employment, for what that was worth.

The image of the Lancaster and its guns he could not bury. 'Why did it come?'

Short answer, and the answer to 'Why am I here, Lord?' — God knows. Certainly somebody did, it was the 'Who?' which niggled.

Gavin resembled his dad in looks — apart from a scar at the corner of his mouth where Dad had accidentally hit him with a plastic golf club when Gavin had been seven. His fair hair and predatory features, his sallow complexion, made worse by drugs, lacked vitality. And he needed a wash and shave.

Fast acknowledging there was more to life than screwing in

the dunes and kicking heads, Gavin mooched across the deserted midway. Bat wing doors on Clint's Saloon Bar Cafe whooshed open and closed — there was no breeze. Everything was becalmed, the town devoid of people. Like a Polaroid snap slowly developing each ride, each building more stark, more… *there*. Things you normally take for granted and largely ignore, seemed to grow, to overwhelm his sense of purpose — just what was that? — and serve to give him the heeby-jeebies.

Gears meshed, they turned him round, the hum of machinery at first a groan rising to an unbearable peak of sound. Gavin clamped hands over his ears, and the huge Pirate Galleon moved, it swayed, it gained an eerie momentum. And it forced Gavin's comment of, 'Idiot, only a hurricane could shift that.'

The noise died to a more tolerable grind; a rifle on his stall fell to the floor with a clatter.

'That you, Freddie?' The echo rebounded from metal pillars and prefabricated buildings. A total, absolute silence crept in and held — like on the cliff path.

A wagon on the Fun House ride clacked over the track and Gavin hurried to check it out. 'Freddie, that you, man?' No answer. 'Aw, come on, quit it.'

The car shunted again… without power. Gavin glanced at the fuse boxes to his left fastened to the upright. The switch was set in the OFF position.

His mouth felt dry, a bit like the aftermath of a night's boozing. Still he kept reminding himself it could be imagination, even hallucination. He climbed into the car. The brake was locked on, yet it moved again, sharply, suddenly. The momentum threw him off balance, wedging him between the seat and the car's front. His head rattled the edge, he saw flashing lights… And… and who the fuck was that other fool — not the clown — pointing a gloved finger at him?

'Freddie.' Gavin eased himself up. 'Aw, man, why you wearing goggles?' He giggled now. 'Storm brewing?'

The car slammed forward, hit the doors, conveying Gavin into an ill-lit darkness. Together, they rattled down a gradient before bursting into a hall of mirrors, his reflection unrecognisable, and multiplied endless times.

Distorted faces all laughed and yelled, Gavin still positive Freddie was behind the joke. Some joke? Fred had to be high to think this one out. 'Excellent, Fred,' he congratulated. 'Absolutely ace.'

He stopped laughing when the image in the goggles appeared. Gavin fell back, hurting inside because he knew it was the same image he had seen at the controls of the bomber... and dementia set in when the gloved hand reached and jerked him upwards.

Flung sideways as the vehicle canted left, he fought to rid himself of the grip on his sweatshirt. The car trembled, the incline dipped alarmingly, the impetus throwing him forward, the material tight about his neck.

Gavin wanted freedom, anything. He would give... anything, even his soul if he could just escape this bad dream. What really bothered him was the fact he knew it wasn't Freddie behind this game.

Tearing frantically at the shirt, buttons pinging into a darkness lit by sickly amber light, he fell the opposite way, the ninety degree turn hurling his brain and stomach into congealed shadows, black amorphous shapes tacked to the walls and ceiling.

The light faded to green, to purple, to red, and then some moron put the bloody lights out.

A deep, dank unsettling night descended, fumes clogged his throat. He wanted to pray but could not find the words.

Air billowed. WHY ME LORD? hung there, the car

collecting yet more speed as vicious shrieks raped the air, and ghosts skated from the darkness.

Gavin tore off the shirt; blood rushed into his ears, his own heart beating the same hideous cadence as the drumming wheels. His sweat dried, he was cold, freezing. Here were pictures of his parents' home in the West Midlands; of his Mother setting border plants; Dad mowing the lawn. Through a window a picture of himself, happy. On the wall the photos of war planes — legacy of a Grandad he had never known. All of this flicked through his mind — his life suddenly that of a drowning man…

He couldn't breathe; seaweed clung to his face. He fought for air… eyes locked on dials… row after row of dials… and the hands before him… his own?… were encased in black gloves.

ESCAPE. The word sat like a hedgehog in the road. And Gavin wanted to reach home before the truck came and squashed it flat.

'I. Am. Home.' This realisation was something new. Because HOME meant he was in the grip of an awesome, incomprehensible power.

Here was salt and sea and six other beings… the drone of heavy engines… a sensation of climbing and the song… Dear lord, the song…

'We'll meet again, Don't know where…' On. And on. And on. And 'JANEEEEE,' was the last word he yelled.

'The girl. Is. Mine.' The voice. The goggles. The laughter of death as he looked it full in the face. And to Gavin it sounded just like a clown.

When the singing died there was nothing. Only the silence of the drowned plane, of others hanging from harnesses, dark sockets staring from behind cracked goggles.

Here was Destiny, pictures from Grandad's collection, all

about him, flooding his drowned brain. One port engine stammered and cut out —

Why is it so cold?

— the engine refusing to be coaxed, the prop spinning, dying. Fish swam through a bullet rent in the canopy, and he knew he was lost, three other props churning water, stammering, finally stilled. And the date on the navigator's calendar said JUNE 19, 1943.

The Fun House doors opened, sea water dripped on the board walk, bright eyes gazed from behind goggles. Mel Cross grinned with Gavin's lips. He rather liked the scratched Doc's he was wearing.

Here was the second coming: RECLAMATION.

Tibb's Cove whispered around him as he left the funfair and passed through a maze of streets he'd last seen during the war. But it was of little consequence, for Cross was making for the one place he would be welcome, the place he knew like a lover knows a partner's body — Hatcher's Field. And the reunion.

He thought about Moon. This time everything would be as it should be without playing with electronic toys.

Time was theirs. His. They were back. A name from yesterday and today curled and he shouted out: 'PURDYYY!'

Suddenly, he was everyone, the brittle skin of his face remoulded. He pictured a cottage where he used to meet Emily: today a girl waved. 'Mattie,' his new voice said.

He studied his image in a shop window, his leather jacket hardly out of place. The transition had been easy, just like 'Alice', he told himself. And she had grown very small, and very tall. Oooh, there was really no end to his talents. Hadn't his dark desires made it possible? They had done it once, had risen from the sea, when? Why in 1954, from the drowned GRUMPY to which they had been condemned all because of some mad experiments, and the shock waves they had caused. Damn fools never realised what it could do to returning bombers. But he knew who was behind those. They had been robbed of life, and it was time to really set the balance right.

Hadn't they caused havoc? Sure they had, and well deserved in this place. They would remember Cross this time, hell they'd never forget him again. NEVER. And he would find Purdy, because he, Cross, was no longer simply a shadow of his former self.

Freddie scratched his shaven head as he stood before the Fun House. Lowering clouds damped down on the Pleasure Beach, the town, everywhere.

'Bloody dark all of a sudden. An' why 'ave all the lights come on? Ain't a bloody eclipse. Jesus, it's on'y ten to three.'

Sure, he'd been snatching some z's under the Waltzer, and if the clown's laughing hadn't woken him, he'd still be there.

Startled, Freddie spun round as a car thundered through the Fun House doors, the doors slammed back, and yet another grinning, painted clown stared at him. 'HELLFIRE...What—?' A torn sweat shirt hung like a limp flag from a section of loose metal on the car. Freddie retrieved it and read Gavin's name stencilled on the pocket.

He grinned. 'Silly idiot's playin' the twat again.' The clown tittered.

Freddie dropped the shirt, and hurried away, something he couldn't rightly say what, placing a cold, hard ball of fear in his chest. He had never liked the Fun House. Nor had many of the others who'd worked it. Something out of kilter in there, they said.

In any case who wanted a dripping, seaweed infested shirt for a trophy?

Freddie ran: the clown shrieked.

CHAPTER 13

Tom Sheridan studied Frank with unblinking grey eyes. He'd listened without comment to Frank's account of Johnny's night-time terrors. Niceties kicked into touch, Frank had used baser language to hammer home his fears.

'I've seen some pretty bad depressions in you over the years, Frankie,' Tom said, 'especially after Marie upped and left, but this one wins the medal.'

Coming home after the war, setting up the shellfish stall, spinning yarns, Tom had tried to retain his old sparkle. Difficult, due to the fact that even then events had seemed to be gearing up for an action replay. Tom had existed on the edge of reality, just over that line of reason he was sure there existed things he knew couldn't be possible. Now, today, he knew different. 'Full circle,' he told himself, 'it's come full circle.'

'You look like shit,' he said to Frank and shoved an untouched plate of toast and marmalade towards his son. 'Gotta eat, lad.' He shrugged at Frank's headshake. 'Where's John?' he asked.

'I left him in bed, he's shattered.'

Aye, aren't we all, Tom thought. The years rolled away bringing back pleasant memories of how he would sit with Frank after his mother had died, trying to be right, to make jokes, the hurt hard to displace. Facing up to his own grief as well as coping with Frank's hadn't been easy, simple definitions about life and death hardly credible. Good men had died in the war, their memories left in wartime huts, their shapes hovering by the planes they had known. It had been hard to convince Frank his mother had really gone.

'Dad,' Frank eventually said, 'I don't know what John saw but what he told me scared the hell outta me. Our Charlie's different again, he's so laid back it isn't true. Like he wasn't even involved. If Marie was here —'

'Frank, Marie's gone.' Tom shoved the chair back and went to make some fresh coffee. Through the serving hatch, he saw the model Lancaster sitting on the polished dining table where Frank had left it. He refrained from comment. Nor did he mention the Rolls Royce he had noticed easing away from the kerb when he arrived, its registration **F M 1** forcing him to spit.

Links had been formed, his own life tied to that last bombing raid, and the terrible realisation as to what had caused it. He knew something bad had returned, and was out there, waiting. He'd become aware of it two nights ago. Packing up the stall, the sudden atmospheric change had struck him a physical blow, everywhere charged with the same force he and the others had felt when the bombers had come limping home on a wing and a prayer — a force such that he wished to God he had never returned.

Cross. Oh yes, it had to be him, had said on that last return: 'Wouldn't it be great to put the shits up everyone in The Cove?'

Jesus! A suggestion then brought to a kind of grim reality forty-odd years on. But it isn't the suggestion, Tommy, is it? he reminded himself. No way it isn't. This is Cross's revenge. Swine wanted his life back. *Or his soul.*

Five of Grumpy's crew hadn't returned, these plus two other bomber crews made up a deficit which should never have been. Nineteen men gone, and it left Tom Sheridan to carry his own badge of self-confessed cowardice because he'd baled out.

He sat down with the fresh coffee, and noted Frank's open-mouthed awe as he spoke.

'"Gunner Purdy" had spotted a Junka, the message going out as we swung over the Dutch coast at near midnight. One port and one starboard engine had failed. We still had a payload because the bomb doors had malfunctioned. Me an' Purdy damn near froze to death trying to release 'em. Over the water we saw the fighter coned by searchlights, flak bursting like on bonfire night. It fired off a red and white flare to confuse the allies, the searchies flicked off, and the flak stopped. A minute or so later I heard Cross warning us that an FE190 was coming at us. We couldn't shake the sod. Bullets strafed us stem to stern, half the tail-fin fell off, and Cross yelled: "ABANDON AIRCRAFT. BALE OUT. LOSING HER. CAN'T HOLD THE MOTHER—" like he was demented.

'Then we felt the heat, Frank. Came over us in waves. Oh, I'd heard rumours 'bout boffins messin' with things but I never paid no mind. Didn't give it a thought 'cos I was scared, Frankie, real, gut-churning scared. I didn't wanna die, nor did any of us, so I went, lad. I followed orders and baled out. It's something I never told a living soul, an' I spent all this time regretting it.'

Tom wrung his hands. 'I'd like to smash that there model. Never should've made it. A bloody Jonah is that.' He shoved a coffee towards Frank. 'Drink up, I laced it with whisky. Reckon we need it.'

'I could do with the bottle.' Frank's smile was feeble. 'I feel like I've fought a war with our Johnny. And now this lot from you. You're a dark horse an' no mistake.'

'Feeling my years, lad,' Tom answered. 'Guess my lease on life, bought at the expense of others, is about up. There comes a time when each of us 'as to unburden our souls as it were.' He sniffled, and scoured his big nose with a spotted handkerchief. 'Even tried tellin' myself I was following orders, but orders ain't nothin' when the flamin' thing comes back like a ghost.' His pause was an angry one. 'One thing I'm certain of is that there bomber has a crew from hell flying it.'

He supped coffee, smacked his lips, and wiped off the residue on the handkerchief. 'Bit unfair is that, an' I'll tell you why… there's only one demon on that plane, and that's Melville Cross.'

Tom leaned across the table. 'D'you know what Cross said that night, Frankie? He said: "*No war, and no scientists can destroy me.*" Said the very minute I baled out, so it goes t'show I haven't laid any ghosts by buildin' that Grumpy model.'

'Been reading about "Snow White" have we?' Frank attempted flippancy to ease the tangible tension.

'Nah, just thinking aloud.'

'What do I do, Dad?'

'Let Johnny sleep for starters. Then I'll take him for a long walk, have a talk with him.'

'Hold on, I don't want you filling his mind with more tales.'

Tom patted Frank's hand. 'Trust me, lad, I haven't let you down yet.'

'Give over, Dad. I'm not questioning that. It's the lads, they're so vulnerable. What's more, they are lads. Charlie's gone off on his bike somewhere. I couldn't stop him. Christ, his head's full of bombers and war and…'

'Whoa, Frank, calm down and quit worryin'. I raised you, so I know what being a father's like.'

Frank felt real uneasy, knowing he should do something, the

problems sitting like an urgent letter yet to be written. 'Dad, just set John right. Tell him it was a dream. Tell him plane's don't come back and shoot people.'

'Wish I could, Frank. ' Tom met his son's eyes, saw the hurt and the puzzlement there. 'Seems I can't tell fibs, lad. If I told our John that, he'd know I was lying. Christ, Frank, he saw the bloody bomber. That isn't no dream now, is it? Aye, John and about two thousand others, they all saw it.

'And think on, it isn't the plane at fault, it's Cross. That mad cowboy's up to something.'

Trust had been destroyed in Tom's memory. Back then he worked with a fine crew so what had happened? What diabolical change had taken place for Cross to have the power to return. *Had to be the fooling around at Hatcher's Field*. HAD TO BE.

He thought about the Rolls again, about what he knew about Moon, but decided to let it lie. For the time being.

Then Marie had come along, and Tom really did think about her, about what she had meant to Frank. The change in her had been profound, all smiles, dressed to kill, and Tom was wishing he'd spanked her behind for her. What good would it have done? He slapped the table, collected his walking stick. About to leave, he paused at the door.

Frank stopped him cold. 'What do you know about Moon?'

Tom picked at the loose ferrule on his stick. 'Why?' Should he tell him about Marie? The link?

'Just tales,' Frank said, rattling the marmalade knife on the edge of the pot. 'Tales about how nobody ever sees Moon, yet every-damn-thing runs like clockwork. Like—' He paused, a tad unsure, then added: 'Like everything is pre-programmed.' He sought an answer from Tom and didn't receive the right one.

'He works from home as far as I know,' said Tom being

evasive, a multitude of secrets vying to be released.

Frank threw the knife down, they both watched it fall to the floor and spin. 'So how come he was involved with those lads who visited the airfield in '54? I heard Moon instigated the whole thing. Dad, open up here, level with me. It's like Moon has some power over us, and the whole town. Nobody goes near Hatcher's, not then, not now.'

Tom sat again. 'Frank, you're as obstinate as I am.' He retrieved the knife. 'Bad luck to spin a knife.' He set it on the plate. 'Who told you about Moon?' Silence. 'Frank, you got on this tack so you talk to me as well.'

Frank walked to the hall door and listened.

'Johnny will be fine,' Tom said, 'so quit acting like a mother hen and sit. I need t'say somethin' which needs no interruptions.'

Frank did sit: he did listen as Tom told him about the aborted mission in '43. And of the names in the Roll Call of Honour at the church. 'We never went to Berlin, lad. Somebody fetched us back, and there isn't no honour in that. See there was this kind of heat force which appeared to radiate from our coastline, and it's something I haven't quite got straight in my head yet.

'Fact is, Grumpy went missing somewhere between the Dutch coast and Tibb's Cove. Two of us, me and O'Connell jumped. Coastguard picked me out of the sea half-dead two days later. Not many get a second chance, Frank, not many at all.'

'So, what's it to do with us? I'm a worker, a fun-lovin' guy when I get the chance. Man, they say truth is stranger than fiction, but this takes the biscuit.' He glanced at Tom. 'Don't take me for an idiot, Dad.'

'Do I ever? Just hear me out. I know that bomber came down in the sea because there's no record of it landing at

Hatcher's Field. And from what I've said, it bloody couldn't on account o' some prats messing wi' things which they thought might turn the tide in our favour. Y'know bring the war, at least the air war, to a close a mite quicker.

'Believe me, Frank, I checked every damn record there is to check.'

The pause was heavy, each of them filled with a mounting dread.

'Somebody high up in the pecking order was acting cagey over it,' Tom added. 'And another thing, Moon, as young as he was, had friends in high places even then. Taught him a lot they did. And don't ask how I know, I just do.'

CHAPTER 14

'Big deal,' scorned Frank. 'Three bombers crash into the sea, but what I want to know is how can one come back?'

A chesty sigh shook Tom's frame. 'Before I jumped — and before you start prattling, I'm gonna finish it, so listen. Thanks. Before I jumped, Cross left it to O'Connell to go back and check the real damage. That plane was as black as a coal cellar, and poor Arthur breathing like he was fighting for air, aye, even through his face-mask. And then he barked his shins on the for'ard bulkhead. Christ, it was cold.

'Cross steered the plane as best he could, a better word would be "fought". That's it, he fought the bloody thing, the whole shebang rattling like the time they pulled down that tin shack behind the old Plaza cinema, recall?'

Frank ignored it. 'O'Connell was killed the other night, Dad. That's important, because I'm thinking has somebody got it in for you? Come on, Tommy, let's hear it all.'

Tom scratched his wiry, grey hair. A false teeth smile came and went. 'Concerned, eh? Think I've got that there senile dementia? Or is something else gnawin' at you?'

'Don't talk daft. I'm just worried. And don't laugh like I was mad, either.'

'Frank, Art O'Connell was a loner. So long as he had bacca

and ale money he didn't give a flying fuck for anybody. His Irish ditties kept the punters happy, and his lobsters lightened their wallets. Art made a livin'. Oh I know most stayed clear of his cottage, claimed he was a brick short. Talked with spirits, they said. Aye, he did, out of a chuffin' bottle.'

'TOM, you're waffling. Arthur's dead. Are you next? Can't do anything about Arthur, but I can sure have a try at protecting you.'

Tom rapped the table with his knuckles. 'O'Connell discovered the mid-upper gunner dead, his right foot shot off and damn near half his left leg. He was froze in his perch, lad, like a chicken on a hook. In the tail, Joe Dykes — that's Jerry Purdy's mate's Dad — was as cold as the ice forming inside that plane. The top of his head had gone.

'George Purdy wasn't too well off either. George used t'put the screamin' 'ab-dabs up his lad about them three gnomes he planted in the garden. Tormented Jerry rotten he did. And his missus. Surprised she stuck with him that long. Don't know what happened to George. I guess he's food for the fishes.'

'Bit gloomy in here,' said Frank.

Tom didn't respond because he knew why. It was time the lights went out, just as they had that night in the grim darkness of the bomber.

'Grumpy, Doc and Dopey, not three of the seven dwarves, Frank, but bombers, all lost that night.' Tom snapped his fingers. 'There... and gone. Nineteen men, just... gone.'

'Dad, listen to yourself.' Frank poured more coffee. 'Let's have that flask you keep tucked away.'

He took the flask and poured a liberal dose in each cup. 'Sceptic I might be, but something tells me this is a load of balls. War is one big slaughterhouse, a culling of the masses. It's full of mad idiots experimenting, daring one another to push another button. There's nuclear accidents, Chernobyl for one, half of that populace still waiting to die.'

'P'raps they already have,' interrupted Tom, 'and just don't know it yet.'

'Another riddle?' Frank drank half his coffee, his cheeks suffused, his face less cheerless.

'They do say,' said Tom, 'that men in battle when they're shot, just keep on running, the brain refusing to accept the body is dead. Who's to say it didn't happen to those three planes? Maybe all those aircrew were dead and didn't know it.'

Sarcastically, Frank said: 'And you, too? Talk sense. I can touch you, you're as real as me.'

'Or as real as somebody wants us to believe.'

Frank's chair creaked as he leaned back, his hands thrown in the air. 'There you go, all crap. Just tell me one thing, who was the front gunner in Grumpy?'

Tom's eyebrows shot up. 'Ah, so I have hooked you. Now you think on that life and death are as close as that knife to butter. Life's a miniature death every time we breathe pollution, or get scared. Every heartbeat's a step closer to the end. What we don't know is… is it the end?'

A draught eased under the door, and Tom shivered. He was in the plane, the cold tying him to that last spoken fear. But then had come the heat — cold heat in which they had sweated, had felt as though they were being cooked, but still their breath had cauterised the air.

'A flyin' coffin is what it was, Frank. Cross and a bloke named Pountney prevented her from stalling. Search lights coned us then everything went black. No Bomber's Moon that night, and hardly any fuel left. Frank, it really was like they were all dead and just waitin' for confirmation of the fact. That's when I went out, I'd had enough.

'A void, falling, praying for a quick end, or a quick rescue. And no, I ain't dead, but I was more a corpse than anything living when they dragged me out.'

'This is the first time you've opened up, Dad.' Frank squeezed Tom's arm. 'Thanks for the trust. But why now? What has it to do with…? Dad, *who was the front gunner?*'

Tom avoided his son's gaze: he looked through the hatch at the Lancaster once more. 'The same guy who led those lads a merry dance in '54.'

'Who? Moon? Aw, come on. If he went down with the bloody plane then how can he —?'

'Soldiers in battle, Frankie. What did I pre-suppose?'

'Nah, it's so… It's too heavy, Dad. It's like stating all of us are allowed borrowed time. That we're living on it.'

'What do you suppose ghosts are, Frank? Memories we don't want to let go? Or something we can never understand? Whatever they are, we sure got a load of 'em in Tibb's Cove.'

'Front gunner has to be Moon's father, his grandad, his older brother.'

Should he tell him now, Tom was thinking, his conscience waging a new war. Tell him about Marie? About the link? After all, it was way past time, and dammit, it was something he should have told Frank years ago.

Tom bit the bullet. 'D'you know why Marie left you to look after the twins?'

'What are you on about? 'Course I know. She couldn't cope, threw a bloody wobbler and walked out.'

'Wrong!' Frank's flinty stare unnerved him a little. 'Marie left because she couldn't tell you that you're not the twins' father, Frank.'

'Bull… *shit*.' Frank, enraged followed it with, 'If you weren't my Dad I'd clobber you for that.'

'Calm down, hear it for what it is, then judge. Think back to the bad patch you and Marie were going through. It was plain she didn't give a owl's hoot in a wood for you. Always down at

Hatters mingling with the smart set. Half-arsed bunch o' lunatics the lot of 'em. Hell, Frank, she was seen by everybody 'cept you. Oh, I know you heard gossip and like the dutiful husband who never thought bad of anybody, least of all your own wife, you chose to ignore it. Don't forget I was bunking here then. Walls aren't exactly lined with lead. But it wasn't none o' my business. Marie was your wife, but because The Cove was in limbo, and had been for years, she wanted some life. So, where does she go? Hatters.

'Frank, none of us are going anywhere. Bus trips bring outsiders to see the wreckage of yesterday, the Tibb's Cove antiques road show. Writing's on the wall, lad. It's fate. Dykes is dead, just like his old man. Soon it'll be Purdy's turn, *just like his old man.*' Tom eased forward again, palms flat on the table. 'And Marie got caught in the back of a big car. Moon is the twins' father, that's why they're reprobates. Neither you or me can do anythin' with 'em. Look at that bruise Johnny fetched you —'

'He was having a nightmare.'

'Sure he was, but it weren't no real dream, it was a throwback memory to days lived by his father. Penny tumbled? Soldiers not believing they're dead, or that their earthly body is no bloody use. Wise up, Frank, you know it's true.'

Tom's need to make Frank understand was more important now than at any other time, for time was nearly up. This argument turned unreal into real, and make believe into slowly developing negatives in the darkroom of the mind.

'You hid your head, Frank. Marie left you holdin' the babies in their *real* Father's town. And the front gunner in Grumpy was *the* Franklyn Moon. Not his kin, but *him.*'

The pin, had it dropped, would have sounded like a steel girder on concrete, Frank aware now that riddles very often had answers... once you tapped the vein.

'We're living on borrowed time, Frank,' Tom said very slowly. 'All courtesy of Moon, and his meddling. Whatever deals he's made, he knows who to make 'em with. He lays down the rules —'

'RULES,' Frank bellowed. Cups clattered, the knife slid again. To hell with it spinning. 'What effin rules? How can a man who should, by rights, be dead, drive around in a Rolls, own half the town, and force six other teenagers into Hatcher's Field? God, he was the same age in nineteen fifty whatever...'

'Fifty-Four. He's here to make amends for a tragic mistake he was instrumental in perpetrating back in '43. Sure he was the front gunner, but I have it on good authority that he laid down the game plan for those experiments —'

'Experiments! Christ Almighty —' Frank was up and pacing, '— all I hear is that word "experiments".' He stood over Tom. 'What experiments? tell me about 'em an' then I can p'raps begin to see what the hell you're talking about.'

Tom waived — to Frank — a frustrating hand. 'Dreams and stories, writ down memories if you will, are a part of it. We're nurtured on 'em. Nobody wants to die, son, not in wars or by natural causes. Think on, so much to live for, that force cut off, snuffed out. Souls floating in the ether, just like me floatin' on that parachute not knowing where or even if I'd land in one piece.

'I made it, Frank. I came back to you, your mam, God rest her, and to this town. I've spent the time wonderin' why I had to land back here? We like to think we're all masters of our own destiny but it don't change the fact that we need others to guide us, but under a set of laws we can all understand.'

'Like God, you mean?' Frank put in. 'Trouble is, even He can't set things right.'

'Don't kid yourself, Frank, everything is pre-ordained, and pre-programmed. You said it, lad, and nobody gets off the ride unless they really want to. Your mam did.'

'What's that mean? Mam's dead, end of story.'

Tom's sigh hung. 'You haven't heard me, Frank. Not one bloody word has gotten into that closed mind, has it?'

'Coming the high an' mighty now, are we?'

Tom gripped his stick, knuckles bloodless. 'I could belt you, you hard-headed idiot. If that's how you want to see things then yes, your old dad is shoutin' the odds, and he desperately wants his only son to understand before it's too late.'

Frank couldn't climb down. He should, and knew it, but he was convinced old age was getting the better of Tom. He wanted to hug him and daren't. Somehow the barriers had become immense brought about by a cockeyed diatribe about the living and the dead, and the real question: which were which?

Tom supped cold coffee, pulling a face as it went down. He wondered if he was the voice of one crying into a void of self-doubt and unreason, or was he merely waiting for the past to catch up and become a new future?

He had heard the song beneath the barnacle encrusted stanchions of the pier —

We'll meet again, don't know where... — in a flat, monotone seeping from the halls of the dead.

Clearing his throat, he said quietly: 'Your mother didn't want to come back, son, because she believed that when you die, that's it. Belief is a strange animal, Frank, the more we try and accept, the more intransigent things become. Your Mam believed that in death, the soul dies too.'

He leaned forward, resting his chin on his stick. 'I'm here to tell you it doesn't. Rebirth, Frank. Pregnancies all over the world. And the stillborn? Not ready. Freaks? Life's castaways. The good, the bad, and every other bloody nonentity struggle to get back, to retain a hold on life. They're the *believers*, laddie.'

The word stung Frank. What, in God's name, were the twins? He loathed that word freaks, too.

'Where do you fit into the grand plan, Dad?' Frank genuinely wanted to know, bound now to its seriousness. It wasn't waffle, the ravings of a senile old man, not any more. Dad wouldn't have brought Mam into it given how much they had both loved her. 'And I'm sorry I blew steam.'

'Aye, right, an' so am I, Frank, real sorry. As to where do I fit y'might say I was given another chance and took the bugger. I came home. I can wait. Nowhere else to go is there?'

'So, are they looking for you to make up the team?'

Rheumy grey eyes said everything and nothing. Frank knew Tom would tell him the rest when he was ready.

'I suppose,' Frank said, 'you should know it wasn't Moon came here in the fancy car. It was that fairground lad, Gavin something or other.' Frank paused, then said: 'Funny thing, he talked in a southern American drawl.' Another pause in which Frank noted how his father's face turned paler. He didn't comment, unsure whether he wished to know or not. 'He left this with me. Told me to show it to you.'

Tom's fingers trembled slightly as he took the creased card from Frank. He read in his gravelly voice: 'Hatcher's Field. June Nineteenth. Reunion.'

Tom studied it for interminable seconds before his braying laugh contradicted his earlier pallor. Frank joined in, he couldn't help it, for Dad's laugh pre-empted any misgivings: it was infectious, and besides, it helped.

'It's Cross,' Tom said between guffaws. 'He always loved a joke.'

'What do you mean?'

Tom wiped tears from his eyes. 'It means you believe it or you don't.' He sniffled, snorted, and allowed his gaze to take on a more brittle, harder edge. 'It really means he wants to set things right as he said he would. Death isn't a barrier, Frank, it's a frontier. So help me, Cross has lifted the gate. He's found the way.' Tom's pause was profound. 'He's coming back a mite late, that's all, to redress the balance.'

CHAPTER 15

Jaqui Dykes crawled from sleep, her tongue like leather, and her bladder demanding release.

Confused as to why it was so dark, she argued she couldn't have slept the clock round. 'I wasn't that drunk.' At the bedroom door, a dull throb at her temples contradicted the fact.

In the bathroom, she eventually managed to splash herself with cold water. An alien face stared back from the mirror, one she loathed, behind her puffy eyes the memory of Dykes, of his destruction.

Shrugging into his dressing gown, she came down the stairs slowly, every step jarring her skull. The hall floor was cold on her bare feet, likewise the kitchen tiles, but she managed to set the jug kettle to boil.

At least it was something to do. Make tea. Teabag? Yes. In the cup. Pour the water, dunk the bag. Milk? Ah, better. It took the taste of sleep and booze away.

The wall clock said a little after three thirty. It was ten minutes fast, always had been, ever since Dykes had bought it from a guy in a pub, where else?

'Aw hell, Dykes, you always made the tea in the morning.'

Outside, an unreal semi-darkness battened the day, patches

of indigo barely brightening the wan, sooty clouds. With her drink, Jaqui wandered into a lounge smelling of Dykes's cigars. His red and black sweater, bought by her last Christmas, was where he'd left it over the back of his chair. She held it to her face, breathed him in. His tatty slippers sat by the cold fireplace beside her dried flower arrangement. Traffic whooshed past. A lot of it.

'It can't be nearly four in the morning.'

Through the window she saw Marilyn's hubby washing his car. Even he wasn't that stupid. 'It's an occasion when he washes it anyway.'

Disconcerting quiet settled, Jaqui aware of her own breathing and heartbeat. Her tummy gurgled. Perhaps if she ate something she might feel better.

On her second bowl of Shreddies, somebody hammered on the front door. Her spoon jerked throwing cereal and milk across the table, each knock a fresh echo in her head.

'ALL RIGHT, I'M COMING.' She flung back the door ready to hurl a mouthful of abuse, and bit it back when she beheld the round-shouldered, grey-faced Len Wells.

'Len? You look as though you've seen a ghost.'

Towing him in, she helped him off with his coat which she draped over the settee, and settled him in Dykes's leather chair. 'I'll make you a drink.'

From behind the mug of coffee, Len's eyes appeared like those of a startled cat's. 'I didn't put it there, Jaqui. I didn't put the DFC back on Emily's rack. It was… was Cross. Nor did I ask for the invitation…'

'Len, hold on, you're losing me. What medal? Who's Cross? And what invitation?' Jaqui was concerned at how bad Len looked, and wondered where Mattie and Joanna were.

Len looked at the flowers on the hearth. 'Nice those. Did you do the arrangement?'

'Len, what is it? You didn't come all this way to admire my floral expertise.'

Slowly, he placed his cup on the tray on the smoked glass coffee table, and then he began to shake. Tears streamed down his face as he blurted: 'I've lost her, Jaqui. Joanna's gone. She's dead. I... I didn't know what to do. I've been walking since dawn. I... recognised your gate... the name on it... DYKES, so I thought...'

Jaqui had gone cold. Dykes dead, now this. She hugged him. 'Tell me about it. Let me help.' Like the blind leading the blind. Lord, what can I do?... Do? She could listen, her earlier inability to understand replaced by a mounting dread.

'All Em's fault,' Len said. 'I should have had the courage to stop it. Always collecting and telling stories to Jerry, scared him to death she did. Had this thing about old pictures, air force stuff. And Mattie would help her, especially when Emily was so ill. And she used to say she didn't want that woman doing her hair. Imagine, her own daughter. Didn't know who Mattie was at the end, come to that she didn't recognise any of us... except *him*, Melville Cross. But Jaqui...' Len grabbed her hands. 'It took the baby. EMILY TOOK JOANNA'S CHILD.'

'Emily took...? Len, she's dead. Emily is —'

'Accused me of spying on her. Told me to leave her alone, that her life wasn't her own, that I was spying on her. Me? And the trouble at the church with Mattie, all Em's fault. A meddler, that was Emily.'

Jaqui's mind retreated: she did not want this, but how could she turn him away? She felt empty, nothing left, no reserves to draw upon, to even consider an offer of help. 'Different reasons,' she managed in a whisper.

'"*Coming in the dead of night, brother—*"' Len spoke softly, the inference making Jaqui's skin crawl. 'She tormented Jerry with that. *"The dead will rise and take you straight to hell."* she told him.'

Their eyes met briefly. 'Pretty, isn't it?' Len said. 'Just the right thing to say to a kid. And then she'd ask Jerry what he'd seen under his bed, in the closet, even in the bloody greenhouse. *"Things buried just waiting for Jerry to dig in his fingers and uncover them. Take you with them. Grab you and take you"* and then the crazy cow would offer him a biscuit.'

Jaqui fought to restrain herself from running out of the house dressed in Dykes's dressing gown and little else. 'I... I never realised. What can I say? None of this would have made sense before —'

'Before that bloody aeroplane came back and did what it did.' Len gripped the chair arms. 'Emily called him back. Lovers they were, during the war. Goddamn you, Cross.'

Thoughts tumbled, found voice. 'We had no right to go to the Field, none of us. Lord only knows why Jerry did.'

Len threw out a sound midway between a laugh and a sob. 'I guess Jerry didn't want to lose face, his dad being an airman an' all. Jerry hated George, but I feel he thought he still owed him and his memory. Six teenagers looking for kicks, and poor Jerry scared shitless at every shadow.' Len paused. 'There was somebody else, but none of us really saw him. We all jumped at every shadow, at every flapping windsock. Jaqui, it was as though Jerry was expecting something to be waiting for him.'

Jaqui recalled the news clippings she'd found in Dykes's box, the ones she'd discussed with Jerry over the phone. And Jaqui didn't warm to the implications.

'Jaqui, even you must know what George Purdy did to his family.'

'Dykes was Jerry's best mate, Len,' she replied, 'even he said nothing. S'pose we all have our secrets.'

(Like a car accident?)

A curtained quiet found a place, the darkness outside heavier, the day's heat still trapped beneath the enveloping mass of cloud.

'Secrets,' Len echoed scornfully. 'George beat Jerry black and blue. Jerry's mam came weeping to us, and I never dared do a thing to prevent any of what she told us. Emily told me not to interfere. A touch ironic eh?'

'Len, don't reproach yourself.' What could she say?

'Why not? I'm good at it. First Em, then Mattie, now Joanna, with Jerry and his mother thrown in for good measure. Quite a collection. And here's me doing absolutely naff all to set things right.' He caught her staring at him. 'Don't talk to me about reproach, Jaqui, I'm a grand master.'

'You know best, Len. A lot of this doesn't make a deal of sense to me.' Safety in non-comment, Jaqui?

He touched her shoulder, an acknowledgement. 'Thanks for letting me unburden myself, it has helped. And I'm sorry about Dykes. I shouldn't have called on you like this, considering —'

'Let's not dwell on it, if you don't mind.'

'You're right, of course. I suppose if Mattie came home it would help me. That bloody house back there's like a tomb.' He wanted to reach out, to hold onto her but refrained, afraid of how she might take it. His plea lingered: 'I want out, Jaqui, just to pack up and go.'

It could be said they both had the idea at the same time. Len looked at her, the moment's indecision trapped in her eyes. 'What say we do just that, Jaqui? Leave Tibb's Cove to... *to them.*'

The heat was unbearable, the humidity forcing perspiration to dampen her skin beneath the dressing gown. Jaqui's headache still nagged, but became the least of her worries.

'I'll pack a case,' she said.

'Thanks, lass.' Len sounded excited. At least it felt good to be doing something. He watched her go to the door. 'Er, okay if I make another coffee?'

'Help yourself. I need a bath first. And you might like to phone the hospital, check on Jerry.'

CHAPTER 16

Death and the onset of decay gripped Tibb's Cove's empty streets; promenade lights blinked in sullen bursts, and breeze-blown litter slow waltzed on the ruptured road. The bus leaned into a shattered shop front, carnage evident in bloodied, crazed glass and the stiffened corpse of the driver still at the wheel. Six teenagers lay on the pavement, the buzzing of feasting flies overtaken by the distant laugh of a clown. Seaward, the water coughed onto a flat, deserted beach.

Above the town, and from where, on a clear day you could see three other counties, the Cottage Hospital's telephone was ringing. Edna Duffy heard it beyond the double doors of her ward.

The pain in her shoulder was tolerable as she reached for the bell push. No-one came. The phone still rang.

With effort, she managed to sit up and swing out of bed, her cotton nightdress clinging. She dabbed her forehead and face with a tissue. 'Hot. So hot?'

For about a minute she sat, perturbed by a heavy throbbing pain across her chest. Her arm ached dreadfully where the bullet had gouged out flesh and bone. But not to be outdone, to discover what was really happening, and more, why there was hardly anyone about, she blinked and refocused on the ward. Drawing in a deep breath, she told herself she was a doer and to get on with it.

The phone had stopped and she had the awful presentiment she was being watched.

'Sister?' There was certainly someone watching her, near the double doors, heavy shadows making it appear like the figure had no eyes, merely blank, dark holes. 'Sister, please, I have pains in my chest.'

The quiet might have cracked in the heat, as Edna groped her way, bed by empty bed, towards the nurse's station in the centre of the ward.

Why are there beds empty after what happened — ? Thoughts tumbled, everything confused. 'There should be people, patients.' A jar of flowers toppled and smashed as Edna butted the table. Petals floated, the spilled water reeked.

'Dear God... it's changed.' A calendar screamed the legend, 1954.

Edna whirled, the impetus promoting an awful dizziness. 'Sister, please...' Edna took a step backwards from the terrible grimace of the woman still there by the doors. And Edna told herself she knew this woman. The name Wells popped into her mind... 'Yes, you... YOU... Jerry's sister. Emily, that's it. You're Emily.'

Did she detect a nod from the woman?

Edna's hands flew to her own face as she realised Emily Wells nee Purdy had died of a brain tumour in... when...? This was 1954, the calendar said so. If it was, then —

'I should like to go home now, back to my cafe,' Edna said. She felt cool tears on her hot face. 'Perhaps Jerry will come and have his breakfast. I'd like to see him again... we have a lot to talk about...' But Edna realised Jerry Purdy was as lost as she was. She'd wanted to tell him about Moon, and the experiments both during and after the war. She had started to...

Maybe it was the reason they had sent the plane...

'I'm so hot.' Edna slumped onto a chair. Heat... intense heat. Rumours of things on screens, images real and unreal, which weren't possible. Tom Sheridan had told her about it over lunch a long time ago, the time when everything had stood still and Tibb's Cove basked only in itself. But Edna had scoffed, never daring to think that Franklyn Moon had been anything other than a gentleman. Some hot times down at the Club in those days.

But come 1954 the course had altered, all because of that stupid prank at the Field. They had upset the grand order of things which Edna, and perhaps a few others, believed they had been granted.

Dizziness came and went in waves. The overhead bulbs popped. Bulbs? They were strip lights when I... when they...

An object fell on her lap, the grotesque evil of the face on the fob throwing Edna back in the chair. The pain intensified. It leapt across her chest and down her left arm, her fingers drawn into claws, the plaster cast encasing her right arm and shoulder suddenly an overbearing weight.

With great effort, Edna Duffy placed one foot before the other, her bulk swaying from side to side as she reached towards a dead woman. 'Emily, help me?'

Her hands passed straight through the apparition, as she pushed through the doors to lean on the far corridor wall. Edna remained beneath the winking lights, her face distorted like a clown's as she slowly slid down that wall to die.

'I told Edna Duffy about it.' Tom Sheridan studied the ever darkening day. He really should get back to his own place, sort a few things, but he supposed he was doing right.

'Told her what?' It was a bitter question, Frank's mind full of illogical facts, which seemed strangely logical when it came down to it.

'Haunted airfields,' Tom shot back. 'And take that look off your face for starters.'

Frank reached for the whisky bottle on the pine dresser. 'May as well finish this as well. Leftover from Christmas.' He poured one for Tom and drained the rest into his own glass. 'For all this, I feel strangely sober.'

'Aye, and then some, when you hear the rest.' Tom sat opposite Frank. They were in the lounge with its Boots prints and a three-piece suite which needed recovering. 'Scoffing is for fools, Frank. What I've said, what I'm about to say, is real, down home truth — seen and heard!'

Frank remained on the edge of his chair staring into the amber liquid in his glass. 'Right now, Dad,' he said, 'I wish I was somewhere else.' He was thinking of the dancer, her legs wrapped about him, and being on cloud nine. But this was cloud zero with a fucking great bomber hanging above him like the Sword of Damocles.

'So, tell me. I guess we got the rest of the day. We can even open another bottle.'

'Frank, cut it out, flippancy doesn't suit you.'

'Who's being flippant?' Frank stared ahead, and Tom could see the small, scared kid again.

'Control tower,' Tom said, 'at Linton-on-Ouse, haunted. Barrack block at Topcliffe where a guard was confronted by the ghost of an airman. An' there's Culham.' Tom paused, sipped his drink, blew his nose on a grey handkerchief. 'Aye Culham, a more diabolical set of happenin's never took place... 'til Hatcher's Field.

'Weird atmosphere about Culham when I was there in 'Forty-Two. Even the entrance was strange. The old manor, Nuneham Courtney Mansion they called it, frightened one of the guards so much he had to be transferred. Summat there that only his two dogs could detect. Wouldn't venture in either. Two dogs mark you, two! A whole basket of best steak wouldn't have got 'em in there.'

Tom grinned. 'Lewis Carroll picnicked there y'know. It's where he came up with the idea for "Alice in Wonderland".'

'Do tell.'

'Frank! Leave it out. Now where was I?'

'Running alongside the White Rabbit I think.'

'Bollocks. If you can't be serious I'm going.'

'Dad, I'm sorry, but you have to admit it's — Oh hell, just get on with it.'

The look was deprecating. 'Aye, well listen then, and less of the bloody sarcasm.' Tom shifted, and settled again. 'There's spooks in the north wing at Nuneham Courtney, and another walks the path down the side of the house. A maid jumped off the main staircase, but what's worse came after the M.O.D. took over and started their experiments.' Tom slammed his glass on the occasional table between them. 'That's got your attention.'

Annoyed, Frank shouted: 'You never lost it, just don't do that.'

'Experiments, and that's what you want t'know about, isn't it? Done by know-alls, airheads wi' bald heads and bottle bottomed glasses thinkin' they hold all the answers right here —' Tom balled his fist. 'Aye and that's bollocks'n'all. Tamperin' with temperatures they were. Atomic Energy Commission and all that. And what's more, Moon belonged to 'em. In fact I heard some of it was his idea. And they cracked it as well. Set and harnessed a world record of something like one hundred million degrees. Ten times hotter than the sun, Frank. Think about that. *Hotter than hell!*

'And they held it. Nuclear fusion it's called. Source of star energy. *Supernatural* energy. And what you can do with that is anybody's guess. Daresay you could create life with such power.'

'Or bring something back,' Frank uttered before he drained his glass. 'This makes sense in view of what you said about soldiers in battle, dead but their minds still alive. Wartime. Thousands dead and didn't accept it... Coming back. God, I'm hot and bloody cold here. This isn't... Dad, what isn't it? This is Moon, and Cross, and the others. This is...' Frank paused wondering whether to say it. He did. 'This is *rebirth.*'

'Cooking on gas, Frank, if you'll excuse the pun. Out of death comes life.' Tom's tone fell an octave or two. 'Or a semblance of it.' He set down his empty glass to look a tad disappointed that he had emptied it. He sat back. 'Tibb's Cove's population is what? Twenty, twenty-five thousand? And what did happen in '54? Some knows, others don't. Think about this, Frank. Everybody has an aura, a life force. If we go before our time by whatever means, war, accident, then what happens to that life force? The church calls it the soul. I reckon they need to come back—' He was thinking aloud now, and ensuring it made enough sense for his son to accept them. 'Unfinished business... like life draws them.'

Frank warmed to it. 'The concept is interesting, but how? This is reincarnation on a grand scale, it's... frightening.'

'Nah, you're a might off base, lad. What about procreation? Moon took Marie, and others for all I know. To all intents Moon is dead, yet he runs this town —' Tom made a fist again. '— and holds it right here. On and on, different lives, souls reborn in the wombs of the living.'

'Sweet Christ, Dad, that's unholy.'

'As unholy as heart transplants? Lungs? Kidneys?'

'That's different.'

'How is it? Life is life, and most want to hang in there for as long as possible.'

'And what has it to do with Hatcher's Field?'

'Heaven and hell, Frank. Souls captured in limbo. I don't know what's really up there. Those lads found out, but it's like a shutter's been brought down on their minds.'

'By Moon?'

'Could be. Energy has created a pathway, its own way of bringing things back, if you like. If the *will* is strong enough then who are we to argue?'

'The plane?'

Tom nodded.

'But they shot up the town, nearly killed Johnny and Charlie. They did kill the Irishman. And today — Just look at the death toll today, Dad.'

'What was born a joke, a suggestion of Cross's has, for want of a phrase, gotten out of hand. For strength there's weakness, son. Animals kill their own, or at best leave 'em to fend for themselves. Only the strong survive, Frank, and that's a fact.' And as if to strengthen his case, Tom added: 'Even if they're dead already, and won't accept it.'

'But why the twins? It could've kill—'

'It didn't. They're strong, have brains…'

'Yeah, they have, Moon's.' The admission, the statement shocked Frank, because he now knew he did *believe*. Frank's threat wasn't lost on Tom. 'I'm gonna finish that crawling swine for good and all.'

He stood with quiet determination, and Tom grabbed him. 'Think, Frank, are you strong? Moon is. He's…'

'Go on say it, Moon's not alive in the accepted sense.'

'I was about to say think about George Purdy.'

'Never knew the man.'

'No, you didn't, but Jerry Purdy did.'

CHAPTER 17

Changes.

Nick Tyler was aware of a takeover, a blip in the order of things, made more evident by the unbearable heat.

He had drunk water in an effort to replace body fluids, his face as he looked down through the window, scalded by Madame Zara's red winking sign. In the distance a muffled explosion: in the streets the stiffening dead. Witnessing change did not mean Nick understood the reasons behind it.

His solitary table lamp flared and went out placing him in a red-strobed darkness. He wondered why his light should go, and not the sign. Pipes rattled as he sought to refill his glass, but the water had gone, dried up, like everything else was in the process of doing.

Mist diffused the sign, it blotted out other lights, it and the encroaching dark lending a surreal, and disturbing taint to the area. Another explosion, nearer this time, caused a selection of paperbacks to tumble and slap the floor. Plaster cracked, becoming a loud, tearing, dust-filled noise, brittle laths forced through the ceiling.

Grabbing a jacket, Tyler tried the door and found it jammed. He thought about Jane, about what an idiot he'd been, and wondered if there might be anything, no matter how small, he could do to make amends. Loneliness, that forever feeling of no-one there to turn to, wasn't in his curriculum.

But computers were. Now, if he could only get to Moon's house. The factory didn't matter, because Nick knew the hub, the centre of the wheel was Moon's home close by Hatcher's Field. Christ, hadn't he been there when he'd come for the interview?

The window did open, and Nick sat on the sill, legs dangling over the mist-filled void. Swinging from the sign's ironwork, he let go to land awkwardly on the cobbled street, a sharp pain running from knee to groin, fetching a cry from him.

He was soaked in sweat as he hobbled the few yards to the mouth of the alley. Angling his head, he was curious at the sound — like an immense kettle kept constantly over heat. Across the road, beyond the railings, Nick dimly made out the sea — it was boiling.

Glass exploded, and he hugged a high wall as storefront windows exploded, shards of glass zinging through the air like... like bullets. He was scared, real sea-boiling scared because Tibb's Cove was undergoing a terrifying transformation before his watering eyes.

Limping down the walkway, he knew he was walking the path to his own destiny, a something initiated a long time ago. He wasn't too sure of the "how?" or the "why?" and had to be content that he was, at least, doing the right thing.

He fought through tubs of lifeless plants, their green foliage fried. Down the road the funfair noise was unreal: Waltzer clacking, Dodgems rattling, and the distorted song was of Vera belting out her message for the brave lads gone to war: 'WE'LL MEET AGAIN —'

The clown's strident, demonic laughter set Nick Tyler running as best he could, the mist closing behind him like a drawn curtain.

Breath ragged, he stumbled and rolled on the grass of the recreation ground, narrowly missing a solid goal post. Beyond it, incandescence, and emboldened by it, the stark shape of a control tower.

Weaving, Nick went towards it, and a large house with tinted windows which stood a half mile to the south of Hatcher's Field.

CHAPTER 18

Jerry Purdy came off the settee uncertain as to what he had heard. He remained uncoordinated for long seconds. Jane Lennard was concerned as she eased up from her own chair.

Their sanctuary was the Purdy house, where a bath and food had given them fresh ability to cope.

O'Leary lay stretched by the hearth, and the ashes of a two day old fire, his short, sharp yelps following Purdy as he lumbered towards the window.

Jane had tried contacting her parents, put out by their non-answer, her Mother's educated tone on the Ansaphone respect-fully requesting the caller to leave their name and number etcetera. Mother was a stranger, a nonentity full of her own self-opinionated charm and bearing. So really the message on the phone had to be out of courtesy, a perpetual underlining of wealth and position. Then again it could be out of a sense of duty, but certainly not to Jane. That had gone out of the window the day she had emerged into this world of... make believe?

Did she care? Did they? Time had been shot to ribbons with indifference and a need to go one's own way. Nicholas was an age ago, her desire faded like the daylight.

Ironically, the telephone's sudden ring was startling. Jane

snatched it up. 'Hello, Jerry Purdy's residence—'

The static emitted from it forced the phone away. The dog nuzzled her free hand, and whimpered.

Jerry had whirled at the ear-splitting screech. 'DROP IT. GET RID OF IT.'

'What was it?'

Jerry was beside her and snatched the phone to slam it back on the cradle, another crack to join the one he'd put there when he'd slung it across the room the day Dykes had died. 'Did anyone say anything, Jane?'

Before she could answer someone rapped at the door. The dog barked once.

'I'll get it.' Jane took a step, only to have Jerry grab her.

The telephone rang again: O'Leary howled, the sound climbing, shredding nerves, Jane begging him to shut up.

And everything did, at once, a clammy, unfeeling silence overlaid by grey shadows held court. It was the same quiet she had experienced in O'Connell's cottage, and Jane knew the dog felt it too.

'Come on.' Purdy steered her upstairs. 'Second room on the left, Mam's old room. It overlooks the front.'

Standing just inside the room with its underlying aroma of perfumes, Jane studied family photographs, the large, heavy furniture, and on the dressing table the formal photo of a heavy set man in uniform, one arm draped about a frail lady with stooping shoulders and pain stitched across a forced smile.

'I don't come in here much,' Jerry whispered in deference to a memory. 'I dust it now and again, but I don't stay 'cos it reminds me of...'

'Your father? Is that what you're trying to tell me?'

She saw the same hardness in his tightening face she had detected on the beach. He was staring at the side of the huge bed where a silent alarm clock sat on a table beside a frilled bedside lamp and a novel by John Buchan.

'My room's the other side. I... I used to hear them through the wall, him and Mam. He kept saying I wasn't any good, that I wasn't a son of his. Mam stood up for me. She told me not to be scared of the dark, or of him.'

He ignored the photograph and drew back the curtain. The front garden was the colour of mildewed cheese, but it wasn't the garden or the withered plants that forced Jerry to bite his knuckles.

'Oh Jane, they're still there.'

Puzzled, Jane looked out. 'What? I can't see anything.'

'They're behind the azaleas, all three of 'em, accusing me.' The mist shimmered in the glow from one solitary street lamp. Purdy squinted into the gloom. 'I can't see them... Oh God, they've gone. GONE.'

O'Leary barked as the knock sounded again.

Without a word, Purdy slammed the bedroom door, the night's sickly light, a prelude to what must come.

In that same, baking, dim light, Jaqui Dykes pulled a face when she inspected the scar in the full length mirror behind the bathroom door. The scar, legacy of her accident, ran from beneath her left breast almost to her groin. 'Dykes gave me the second chance —' She sniffled. 'All past.' She shrugged into a sloppy jumper. 'Life goes on.'

Through her window, the whole of The Cove lay beneath a heat haze unrecorded in scientific study — except maybe one.

Struggling downstairs with one big suitcase, Jaqui said to Len: 'Did you call Jerry?'

Len shrugged. 'Tried. It just rang out.'

Outside, Len shoved the case in Jaqui's Metro as she settled herself in the driver's seat. The vehicle coughed, it steamed, and wouldn't start.

'SHIT!' Jaqui thumped the dashboard. 'We're not meant to leave, Len.' She had resigned herself to it.

'Don't say that, Jaqui, we have to.' Len sounded scared. 'Let's walk.'

They walked, keeping close, afraid if one strayed they would lose sight of the other. Every breath was hard won, the air seared their lungs.

Len muttered: 'History repeating itself,' and Jaqui hadn't the courage to ask him what he meant.

Hadn't the courage because certain memories, happenings in her life were blank spaces — the accident for one. With a scar like she had, small wonder she hadn't died.

The Air Museum was a recognisable landmark and Jaqui slumped on the seat before it. They had walked for a good half hour, and now all they could hear was the bubbling sea.

The intermittent beam of the lighthouse cut the mist. Screams from the darkness climbed and were gone, heightening her own unease.

'Len, we have to move. We're sitting ducks here. Sorry, but I'm on edge.'

'Know what you mean.' Len collected her case.

"VISIT A REAL AIRFIELD" the sign in the museum window read. The edges of it were charred.

'Came here once with Dykes,' she told Len. 'Only thing I recall is three plastic dummies dressed in flying gear. I ask you.'

She remembered their leather helmets, the goggles, the silk scarves, sheepskin flying jackets and black leather gloves — *exactly like the ones she stared at now as they walked out of the mist.*

'LEN! LEN! RUN, DAMMIT, RUNNNN.'

From halfway up the steep cobbled street, the church bell tolled, this particular emergency bell not sounded since 1954, and before that, when the bombers came home.

But the trio went past them, faces behind goggles and scarves set, like they knew just where their destination lay.

There was something in the shadows by the wardrobe, and Jerry backed nervously away.

Jane Lennard wondered what he was doing. And she uttered a little yelp as the picture frame fell over. Then she glued herself to the door as the bedclothes writhed.

The clamour at the front door rose in intensity, along with O'Leary's howls. Then the downstairs door flew off its hinges. Jerry nearly ripped the curtains off their track in his panic to look through the window, the mist parted just long enough for him to see that the three gnomes really had gone, and that his eyes hadn't deceived him.

And right now Jerry Purdy witnessed three airmen standing on the lawn.

He nearly wet himself, yet it wasn't that which scared him, it was the fact that something else was shoving a way up through the soil… beyond the azaleas.

'GET OUT.' Purdy shoved Jane onto the landing, through his own room and jerked open the window. Without finesse, he forced Jane out of it and onto the flat roof of the kitchen.

Three sets of footfalls sounded on the stairs.

He was wedged in the window. 'JANE, PULL. FOR CHRIS-SAKES PULL!'

He fell, taking the brunt of it on his injured arm as he hit the roof. 'The water butt,' he hissed between clenched teeth, the pain making him giddy. 'Quick, lower yourself onto the edge of the barrel. There's a ladder by the greenhouse, fetch it. And HURRY. Please…' he whispered as he watched her disappear into the mist.

'I HATED YOU, GEORGE.' His father's face hung there, even as Jane set the short ladder against the lip of the roof.

A gloved hand reached for him even as his own arm slid over the roof and to safety.

Purdy whimpered: 'Tell 'em, Mam. You tell Emmy I didn't mean to do what I did. Moon made us. Tom! Fetch Tom. He knows. He made the model that brought 'em back. Somebody got to switch… SWITCH 'EM ALL OFF. JANE, YOU TELL 'EM. *THAT WAY THEY CAN'T COME BACK.*'

From the other side of Tibb's Cove, Jane heard the surly bell. And from behind heavy clouds issued a teeth chattering drone.

Through dark eye sockets, and from behind a mouldy scarf, the figure watched Nick Tyler as he ran down the lane parallel to Hatcher's Field.

Doc Martens shuffled in the dust.

Other eyes watched from a cottage window.

DESTROY, Nick's mind repeated over and over. And then the other voice said: *'You belong.'*

Someone there, weird light shining through perspex.

He found his voice. 'I DON'T BELONG TO ANYONE.' And wasn't that his trouble because he wouldn't allow himself to be trapped?

Nick kicked out at the figure, but his feet met empty air. The figure was on the other side, by the fence, and it laughed, a sepulchral, water-logged sound before being swallowed by the mist.

Warmth flooded back into Nick, and he ran with a purpose. 'Have to reach the house.'

For Jane Lennard to accept any of this stretched her Bible learning to the limits. Yet, she know after what she had beheld at the beach cottage, seeing *was* accepting.

Her ally was Jerry Purdy, and she his, and perhaps O'Leary, who padded on silent paws as they negotiated the narrow path and climbed the stile to follow the glow.

And from inside the Purdy house someone called Jerry's name.

Frank Sheridan was alone. Charlie hadn't come back. Now, Dad and Johnny weren't here. In Frank's head, one name: MOON.

Shrugging into his leather jacket, Frank ventured out into a town he couldn't recognise anymore. Heat curled and shifted like the heat from bread ovens when he had once worked in the bakery downtown. He walked slowly, hands outstretched before him, totally unsure of his bearings. Once familiar streets had become a maze of solid walls, hedges and fences, all merged, all confusing.

Telling himself to maintain a reasonably straight line, he would meet the promenade, he walked slowly, the road angling downwards.

What is life? he asked himself. And existence? That's all most of us are doing, existing, with no useful purpose. What am I seeing? Hearing? He stopped then. 'Am I fuckin' well creating this? Creating what I wish to see?'

A scientific journal article he'd once read promoted the same premise, that we create things in our mind. So, he was concluding, is it fair to say we conjure our families. Our homes? Are they there only when we wish it? Are we all just a product of another's imagination? Conjuration?

How do dead men walk? *Soldiers in battle, Frank!*

Are we all... ghosts? And what is history other than a documentation of events we are led to believe happened?

'Why is this happening now?' He clung to a lamppost, aware of open windows, of curtains hanging limp against sodden, heat seared walls. Even the stone sweated.

It seemed everything had gone, ceased to be. His wife,

maybe his kids. His life. That, above all. 'Products of mind.'
Frank walked on like he was the only man left on earth... until
he conjured somebody else, that is.

And when, Frankie, does today become tomorrow? Become
yesterday?

Multicoloured lights hung on the mist, and the entity that
was HATTERS climbed out of the grey before him, a Rolls
Royce Camargue parked at the kerb. Frank crossed the road.

CHAPTER 19

'Grandad, are we all going to die?'

Such a profound question from a ten-year-old, mused Tom Sheridan as he leaned on the fence overlooking the Cove.

'We all die sometime, John.'

'I know that, Grandad, but when? Do we know it? Or does it just happen?' Johnny hoisted himself onto the fence to witness the grey blanket being drawn over the town. 'It's a bit like my dream,' he said, 'only in that I was being chased. I thought I was going to die.'

This one's not behind the door, Tom guessed. He knew it would get heavier and he was tired, more now than he had been for years, and especially after the hard time he'd had convincing Frank.

'John,' he said, 'some things are difficult to explain.' What do I say? I can't give him the spiel I gave Frank, Johnny wouldn't buy that. Then again—

'Is our Charlie dead?'

'Don't be daft,' Tom barked, put out by the suddenness of the question. 'Charlie can take care of himself just like you can, like your dad can.' Tom tapped his stick on the fence the rhythm too much like a song he wanted to forget.

'We're all of us here for a purpose, son. Time comes, we go.'

He daren't say sometimes things return. He dare not say that.

'Are me an' Charlie here for a purpose, Grandad?'

Tom wanted to say: Ask your dad, meaning their *real* dad, but shoved his briar pipe between his teeth instead. 'Who knows, Johnny? We can't pre-ordain events (Oh no?) We can only accept 'em for what they are, and do our best to skirt the bad 'uns.'

'What does pre-ord... pre-ordain mean?'

Tom ruffled the lad's hair. 'Full of it, aren't you? It means we can't plan things the way *we* would like to. It's already been laid down as a matter o' course.'

'You mean like me and Charlie planned to hang that dead cat outside Purdy's place? That was meant to be?' Johnny's eyes were like saucers. 'WOW! That's great.'

Tom was angry, he knew the twins were devils, legacy of Moon, but too many other things pressed. Maybe he was looking down on a memory, and talking to a grandson who wasn't true kin.

Wasn't because he had been born from the seed of someone already dead. When he, Tom, had bailed out "more dead than alive" it set him to thinking just who he was talking to — his grandson, Johnny, or a clone of Franklyn Moon. Something cold scrabbled up his back.

Behind them the mist entrapped the derelict hangars of Hatcher's Field.

'I know where Charlie is.' Johnny jumped from the fence.

Tom bit hard on his pipe stem. 'So, tell me.'

Johnny jabbed a finger. 'In there.' He grinned, and Tom hated that grin.

The past was in that grin, memories scrolling like on a computer screen, Tom certain he had been pre-programmed for total recall. Should never have made the model, he told himself. But, like everything else, it was way too late.

'Let's walk.' He ushered Johnny along with his stick, knowing now why he felt scared of the boy.

'Where are we going, Grandad?'

'To find Charlie, where else? Your dad's worried sick.'

The sad, world-weary cottage strolled out of the mist and met them, watery light washing dirty windows, it peeped through dead ivy fronds tacked to grey walls.

The door opened at Tom's knock. He doffed his cap. 'Miss Mattie Wells?'

Her face was haunted and Tom knew it wasn't the same happy-go-lucky girl he used to jaw with by the pier about her forthcoming wedding.

'Er, sorry to bother you, lass, but me an' the lad wondered if we might trouble you for a glass of water. The heat y'know.'

This might have explained the true meaning of pre-ordained, for Tom had planned this no matter what force might be around to prevent it. Tom Sheridan wanted to know who was in the cottage besides Mattie Wells.

Mattie indicated a garden seat. 'Sit there. I'll fetch some lemonade.'

'May we come inside?' Tom said offhandedly, 'perhaps it's cooler.'

'NO!' Abrupt, putting him in his place. 'Please wait here.' The door closed.

They sat, Johnny swinging his denim clad legs. 'We'll never find Charlie in this fog, Grandad.'

Mattie leaned into the door. She felt weak, every moment here a lessening of her resolve, her strength, her life force drained in every bead of perspiration.

Joanna's baby was in its makeshift crib — an old dresser drawer with brass handles — and Mattie dare not venture near it. Dare not because the thing wasn't human. Upstairs, footsteps paced. She heard the creak of bedsprings, the muffled moans of ecstasy.

Mattie shook the thoughts away. 'In my mind, not real. Mother, go away.' She crossed to the pantry and came out with a jug of lemonade which she poured into two glasses. At the base of the stairs, she paused resting the tray on the newel post. Her mind went haywire, her own body lusting for that which she had been too young to appreciate. She looked into a gathered gloom, hearing, seeing — *Emily stretched across the vestry table, rutting with that… that abhuman entity dressed in airforce blues.*

And Mattie mouthed the message scrawled on the photograph:

"Keep it warm. Love… Mel" Oh, and the three kisses. Don't forget those. *And medals jangled. Mother screaming with delight, and Mattie had grabbed the candle and rammed it into the Reverend Black's eye, even as he had rammed his penis between her legs… sticky warmth running down her naked flesh.*

And she had known what it was really like because hadn't Mother reached out with her mind and pulled her in to the union? Even when Mother visited her in her room, told her things about Mel, and what would come to pass. 'And our minds mingling, sweetheart, will pave the way for him. I will be you, and you will be me… *foreverrrr.*'

The home truth kicked her in the stomach, the tray tilting, slowly spiralling, lemonade and glass spilled and shattered across the floor.

In it was reality. And the sound of bombers. She could hear them, just as Mother had during the war.

ALL BECAUSE OF A PROMISE. AND A SUMMONS.

Mattie cried out and flung back the door. Tom Sheridan caught her as she fell against him, though Mattie Wells was still a prisoner of her mother's, of Emily's dead/alive mind, even as Johnny yelled: 'LOOK.'

Landing lights winked on, their hazy glow glimpsed through the rolling fog, circular, flickering ghosts swirling across Hatcher's Field, illuminating a running figure.

Johnny ran to the fence. 'It's Charlie.'

From behind, Mattie Wells said, though not in her own voice: 'Welcome to Hell Night.'

From upstairs in Emily's home away from home, a baby cried, the sound like nothing on this earth.

And Charlie screamed and yelled for help as he tried to get through the wire, his jumper torn, threads left on the fence. 'THEY'RE BACK. FATHER BROUGHT 'EM BACK!'

Tom knew just who he meant.

At the Purdy house something wet slopped across the kitchen floor. A whisper soured the air. It said: 'JERRY!'

The child's voice filled the room, burying the threat from that other voice. It was a voice out of a terrified past, held in the very fabric of the house. And it said:

'*Mam, don't like the dark, nasty things there.*'

Tibb's Cove belched out foetid air.

'*Light the light, Mam.*'

The Cove sweated.

'*Emmy tells tales, Mam. Don't let HIM get me.*'

The Cove put out its arms for the return…

'*Little Miss Muffet*' — A new voice now, a distorted whisper curling out of the murk. '*sat on her tuffet, eating her curds and whey. Along came our Jerry and poked out her cherry, and they all had a wonderful day*'.

Something covered in mud slid up the stairs.

'*Emmy's talkin' dirty, Mam, tellin' tales.*'

The mist grew denser. From the front bedroom issued wet, sickening noises, and whatever had heaved itself from the front garden behind the azaleas stood in the darkness by the wardrobe. It waited. It had plenty of time.

Frank Sheridan pushed through the revolving door of HATTERS, the air enriched with stale booze and tobacco. Chairs were neatly stacked on tables, the gaming machines silent.

Frank stood quite still at the entrance to the vast clubroom, his fists clenched, his shout of: 'MOON!' skittling into every niche.

Blue velvet curtains across the stage shifted slightly; streaked shadows clung to gilt balconies; the bar's grill stayed firmly shut, an emergency light attendant on the optics.

Frank repeated his summons as he negotiated the tables, behind him chairs moved, unseen hands placing them at the tables, but Frank heard nothing.

The bunting read: **WELCOME HOME BOYS** as forms materialised, they occupied seats as Glenn Miller's 'In The Mood' pepped up the quiet. People clapped, cheered, they raised glasses.

Illusion, all of it, a figment of his own self, a conjuration from his imagination. Frank Sheridan had parted the veil from yesterday to seek the man who had ruined his life today.

Music faded, a new, more strident tune "The Stripper" taking over as stage curtains whispered open.

The sexy, Monroe look-alike dancer who had winked at Frank only weeks ago, held every male gaze to her sequined G-string, and to the top hat into which she had squeezed her breasts.

'Ooh Frankie,' she cooed, beckoning with a finger. 'Come and help Carol unfasten her string, baby.'

Slow handclaps, cheers urged him on. Hands patted his back, gave him a gentle shove — he felt them and was unnerved by it — but when he turned to look there was no-one there to have done it.

Carol continued her bump and grind, her buttocks wobbled in time with her revolving breasts. Blonde hair tantalised, red lips pursed for a kiss, the gestures she made urging him to untie the knot, pull the string and take up his options.

It had been a long time.

But the heat was something else: like dry ice, the mist layered the stage, and even as Frank reached to pull the cord on the express which he knew could never stop, he became aware of a sickly-sweet stench of the drowned. He turned quickly and faced an airman.

'Where's Moon?' Frank was blinded by his need to exact revenge, how or why was secondary to his consuming lust to destroy.

Carol's fingers danced up his body, tickled his crotch. Right now, it wasn't what he wanted, and he made to shove her away, his hands bursting through her shoulder flesh to grip the bones beneath. He recoiled, her once baby blue eyes now black holes oozing putrescence.

He drew back his hands, he wanted to puke, the stench intolerable. And the voice, the seductive tone still evident. 'Aw, go on, babe pull the string and get the prize. Take a look at what you're missing.'

'Marie?' God Almighty it was her voice. And Frank's own voice sounded very far away, his gaze reluctantly drawn to the undulating belly of the wife he hadn't seen for over eight years.

The skin swelled, stretched and punctured, the smell putrid, as twin heads eased out, their sickening grins more than he could take as they chorused in unison: 'Hi, Dad.'

But they weren't addressing Frank, they looked beyond him to the man who unwound his scarf, removed a homburg from his head, each faltering step bringing him nearer to Frank.

As the scarf fell to the stage, Frank took a hesitant step backwards and bumped into the woman with sagging breasts and mummified skin.

'I am Moon,' said the voice. 'I heard you call me.' Searing light speared Frank, held him. 'I own Tibb's Cove. I own *you*.' Hands flexed, the skin as old and brittle as a mummy's.

How can I destroy this? Frank was running down possibilities, scared yet for some sick reason, wanting to laugh. So this is the soldier who came out of a battle is it?

'Join the Club,' Moon said, through a mouth full of rotten teeth. The hand grabbed Frank's wrist, pulled him closer. 'I'm tired of this body.' But a look crossed Moon's features, the milky eyes averted, head cocked, like he'd had a thought he should be elsewhere.

Frank felt he was too close, rancid breath washed over him. 'Aw the hell with you.' He lashed out, even as demented laughter circled around him.

He found himself just inside the door inspecting stacked tables and chairs, a curtained stage. 'Dad, I'll kill you,' and the sound of his own voice was welcome relief. 'I didn't go in. I didn't walk to the —'

But something had happened, because when he reached the foyer he chanced to look into his open hand, beyond the segments of ragged flesh still adhering to his fingers. He saw the grinning demon staring up at him from a cracked key fob.

'Am I really here?' He echoed his own questions. 'Am I really me?'

A sudden whoosh of flame singed his hair and the left side of his face, the skin a blistered mess, as HATTERS burned from within, creating its own hell.

Frank hit the revolving doors, and they in turn vomited him onto the wet pavement. From over the road, he watched the place die, and with it, he prayed, Franklyn Moon.

Unfortunately, one question hung and stung: How can you destroy the dead?

CHAPTER 20

The sign read:

ROYAL AIR FORCE
BOMBER COMMAND
HATCHER'S FIELD

Tom Sheridan was home. Or, more aptly, facing up to his responsibilities. He ran fingers over the board's weathered surface, and smiled. Mattie stood with him: they had discussed much, not least the connections, and each, in their own way, had to know the truth, no matter how difficult that might be.

Johnny had found Charlie — the two halves whole once more. Charlie had said little to Tom, but he had to Johnny, and together and a distance away, they appeared to be waiting. Each boy held the same tell-tale smirk, and Tom felt it was like looking in a mirror.

From the cottage, the child in the drawer cried out. Mattie scrubbed the goose bumps from her arms, and stayed close by Tom.

'I'm scared,' she said, not wishing the twins to hear. 'I feel like I'm in church again. Feel so alone with no-one to turn to. Nicholas, he —'

Tom gave her a hug. 'All of us are alone at sometime in our life, Mattie. We all have personal, private decisions to make. We have to find our purpose, lass. Souls in the wilderness, trying to find a way back, that's us.'

Reverend Black's sallow face haunted her: she might never be free, her life one long abuse. And the bidding had started when she was four years old.

The air moved, it shifted, landing lights glowed brighter. The twins danced with glee, aware the lights were a signal. The boys' were on their way.

Len Wells and Jaqui Dykes paused at the very same fence Tom and Johnny had chewed the fat by. They were tired, dehydrated, the oppressive heat offering little or no respite, and it was so much hotter up here, at the Field.

The steep winding road leading west out of The Cove had been impassable, blocked by a massive tumbled oak. Their energy sapped, they had no other recourse than to come back — where they belonged.

Tibb's Cove wanted them, it held them to its bosom.

Len broke off a dried twig and twirled it between his fingers. 'We came this way in '54,' he said. 'All seven of us. We went through the wire beyond Emily's cottage. Fitting in a way, because it's where she scared Jerry to death with them wild stories of hers.'

He stared into the bank of fog, a faraway, bitter look carved into ageing features. 'There was me, your Dykes, Jerry, a guy called Siddal, Moon, naturally, and Pountney.'

'You said seven, Len?' Jaqui expected confirmation.

'Ah, yes —' He was thinking: A bomber crew. Just the right number. (Seven dwarfs all in a row.) He went on: 'The other, er, bloke was someone we could sense rather than see. Kept in the shadows. Not that we gave a toss then, kinda added to the fun you might say. Fun! There's an understatement.'

Again Len stared into the opaqueness, Jaqui thinking he might still be seeking that seventh "bloke". Through the grey, a blotch of rude, purple sky intruded. Without warning, Len grabbed Jaqui and hustled her behind a lowering elm. 'Hear it? Don't you hear it?'

The air hung like stage curtains awaiting the signal to open, it was so still you could cut the heat, the distortion heralding the heavy, sonorous thrum of engines.

The hole in the cloud base grew, the purple streaked with red, marking the silhouette of GRUMPY, roundels dancing in the sudden effusion of light, bomb doors open, the glare bouncing from the perspex canopy.

The wheels were down, burnt rubber welded to the runway as she came in.

That kerosene smell, plus the pungent aroma of salt and seaweed charged the air, the bomber dripped water.

Purdy and Jane saw it, Purdy in the lee of the control tower, Jane clinging to his arm. O'Leary cowered behind her.

The tower became a homing beacon, it beckoned, a moving light swinging left to right just like the torch Dykes carried that night in 1954 when —

Moon told Jerry to break down the control room door so they could see inside. Only this time it was Jane and a dog following him up those well worn concrete steps, and this time the blue door at the top was unlocked.

'Jerry, I'm scared.' She held his hand.

Jerry wasn't listening. He was back in '54. He would lose face if he let the side down, and he couldn't do it again, not after the shot putt fiasco. Besides, he wanted to show Emily that he could do it. He wanted to finger gesture her tales, especially the ugly rumour about the devil being there, watching over his children. And it was the same devil who lived in the greenhouse, the one who would surge up and bear him down to everlasting fire for the coward, the wimp that he was.

And he had to prove it was a lie for George, the father who had belittled and beaten him, the same man who had called him "Coward".

They stood in a line, with Moon, and the feeling, only a feeling, of an unshakable presence in the darker shadows behind. It had been funny, but now, up here actually in the tower, it wasn't.

Consoles shone dully beneath diffused moonlight through opaque glass, a breeze whistled through the fabric. A microphone sat on a table amidst a clutter of maps, and charts; other maps were tacked to the walls alongside a picture of a young Jean Simmons. Trophies stood on shelves, pieces of German planes, a swastika, records of "kills" highlighted with Dykes' torch.

'Just mementos that's all,' Len said. 'Don't know what all the fuss is about, Moon.'

Then the static plastered them all to the wall, hands jammed over their ears. All except Moon that is… and the other.

Left, left, steady, now right… holding, holding…

Jane tried shaking Jerry, wondering why he kept repeating: 'Don't you hear? Don't you hear?'

CLIMB. CLIMB. Standby. Corkscrew starboard. Red tracer. Red Tracer. JESUS! ME109 port… PORT. Coming at us. Attack run… Guns… Somebody get the fucking guns… Christ, so hot. So unbearably hot…

White noise removed the rest.

Jerry stood ashen in the limp light. Dykes had said: 'Bloody hell, come and look here.'

They looked out through the cracked window — Purdy and Jane. Jerry said quietly: 'It's what we did, Jane. Me, Dykes and the others. It's what we were meant to do. Moon made us. Bastard needed t'know if his experiment could work. It didn't in '43. He destroyed 'em all then, but he needed to fulfil his promise to Cross. It wasn't right. I knew it wasn't.' His brain was filled with startling, frightening images, and the thought of what he had done in '54. This was impossible.

'Jerry!' She shook him. 'You're rambling again. What is it you are saying exactly?' Jane threw him a worried glance, then, unable to contain herself, she looked back through the filthy window, still unable to comprehend what she was really seeing.

It is today, her mind repeated, but it was here. Whatever they had done in 1954 she reasoned had to be the catalyst to this. Moon's plan had finally succeeded. And so had Melville Cross's dream.

She stared: they both did, her and Purdy.

It sat on the runway, moonlight striking its camouflaged hugeness. On its nose it had that painting of GRUMPY, with no Snow White to smooth away the irritation, blazing eyes looking out on a world that it hated.

Trucks came and went ferrying equipment through the open maw of a huge hangar — men merely faceless shadows in the half-light.

From the plane, six crew climbed down the ladder.

Purdy blurted, still unsure, still locked in his youth. 'They can't, this is ten years after. THEY CAN'T.'

'Jerry.' Jane was shaking him, trying to make him realise: 'It's NOW, Jerry. Not *ten* years, it's over *forty*. What you're seeing... *isn't there.*'

Then why is the field glowing, Purdy asked himself. I told you the one about the boys going under the wire?

Jane persuaded Purdy down the steps and towards a bank of

rusted, unused anti-aircraft guns, where a tarpaulin flapped crazy wings. They skirted the guns. Purdy halted to peer into a mess of clotted shadow by an air raid shelter.

His arm wearing the pot jerked up like some ill-functioning marionette. 'It's there. Oh God. I SEE IT.'

So did Jane. And it moved slowly towards them. It stopped, the leather of the Doc's on its feet hardly able to support the crumbling from within.

Jane recognised it and mouthed: 'Gavin?' She screamed out, loud and long, fetching Purdy from his decades old nightmare. And because Purdy had realised now was *now*, so too did Cross from behind the eyes of the one he'd possessed.

'You... have... something I need, Purdy.' The voice was disjointed, syllables barely comprehensible, the speech reminiscent of a record played at slow speed.

'I haven't got anything of yours,' Purdy said, defiantly standing his ground. 'You got the wrong Purdy, Cross. You need George, my father. He has it. I know it, because IT'S WHERE I LEFT IT WHEN I BURIED THE BASTARD.' Now the thing was darkness itself, the eyes mere pinpricks of light, and if ever light could be described as black, Purdy and Jane saw it then. The thing bellowed its rage, hands cleaved the air, flesh flying from it, the gloves tearing.

Jerry and Jane ran, as the bomber's mid-upper Browning 303's swivelled, levelled, a bony finger poised on the trigger.

Jerry slammed up against the hangar wall, Jane fighting for breath. They risked a look — ON NOTHING. Jerry let out a blast of breath, and hammered the walls with his fists.

They dropped to the grass when they heard the shots, bullets ricocheting off ground, walls and the miserable white painted stones bordering the overgrown pathway.

Sweat painted Jerry's body: it was getting hotter.

Blazing light issued through cracks in the hangar door,

splayed out like the spokes in an umbrella. They shielded their eyes. The firing stopped.

Purdy fought for breath, his weight the handicap it had always been. 'Jane,' he stammered, 'they shouldn't be... be here. I saw to that in '54. I... I burned 'em.'

Trouble is, Em's words kept repeating inside his head.

Sometimes they come back.

Another thought from God knows where popped into Purdy's fevered, uncomprehending mind, and that was: *Souls crying out to be reborn.*

And that he dare not comprehend.

Peering around the corner, Jerry could see an empty runway, and hear the desultory flap of a windsock. GRUMPY had gone.

Jane tugged at his sweater sleeve. 'Please, let's go.'

'No.' He was adamant. 'There's something I have to do... again.'

That was when the noises started: harsh chuckles as shapes climbed through holes in the mist. The hangar light grew brighter, hotter, it lit abandoned M.O.D. vehicles beneath a clutch of scorched trees.

Jane could not accept it, one word hanging: 'Look.'

The shapes cavorted, faceless nonentities on squat, sexless bodies. Short, fat, stunted, elongated, all smeared in mucous and blood. The unborn. The souls craving rebirth, all set loose from the massive womb which had nurtured them. Warmth, comfort... but now they couldn't wait. Time had switched, their reunion long overdue, like forty-six years overdue.

'NO,' Purdy yelled, 'YOU'RE DEAD. I BURNED YOU IN YOUR WOMB.'

Jane realised he must have flipped, and she again begged him to leave with her. But Purdy was having none of it. He shoved her through the small door into the blazing heat of the hangar. When he came through, Jane had gone.

He screamed for her: it brought no answer. He wasn't lonely with Jane. She couldn't be gone, not now.

The smoke-blackened hangar, legacy of before, was ablaze with arc lights, it hummed with machinery, and it crackled with static...

Nick Tyler surveyed the long room, the crackle of static issuing from a massive bank of computer screens.

He had simply walked into Moon's abode through the massive oak front door, to rediscover this soundless void, so clinical it wasn't true. He remembered his first visit here, the sudden feeling he'd experienced, and he had known then it couldn't be allowed to continue.

It was time to end it. And to begin again.

There was not one stick of furniture in the place, no sense of the house ever having been lived in, yet here he was now faced with... what?

This was something new. Even he hadn't been prepared for this. He did not like it.

He walked the ranks. Sure he'd noticed the swivelling camera eyes, but what the hell, he was here for a purpose, precisely what he wasn't too sure. Maybe to save The Cove. Maybe to win back Jane, the risk of being seen secondary not part of the plan.

He looked at a screen and stopped. He stared at himself staring at himself... at himself. And he saw Len Wells, and a woman he knew as Jaqui huddled behind a tree; Mattie and Tom and the twins by the fence; Frank Sheridan, his face scarred, sitting at his dining table, a hammer raised to strike the model Lancaster before him.

And here was the hospital filled with wounded; people crawling in the streets, moaning, screaming... And Jerry

Purdy looked up at him… And it became so clear. Here was Tibb's Cove, its people, its *lives*, all —

'Entrapment, Mr. Tyler.' The voice was cold, electronically stabilised, but the figure it came from was real, and it stood just inside the door through which Nick had so recently passed.

'Mr. Moon?' The question was rhetorical, Nick knew it was Moon. He was also aware all of this was Moon's doing… Through decades he had *owned* this town… *BODY AND SOUL.*

Nick allowed himself a grin. It was one of reconciliation, for he knew if Moon had meant what he said when he'd offered him the position of software designer, a new order was in the making.

Nick Tyler wasn't too sure he could live with that. Not with Moon in tow.

'We've all lived in limbo,' he said, addressing Moon, the man lingering in shadows which appeared to move with him in the glaring white of the room. 'We all work, play, eat, shit and make love at your behest it appears, *Mister* Moon. I believe you're the fucking rabbit we chased down the hole like bloody lemmings.'

'I can give you a job for life,' Moon had said way back. 'The offer still stands.' Again an echo of that same day when Nick had needed to weigh the pro's and con's. 'You'll never want, Mr. Tyler,' Moon added.

'I won't? And what of twenty odd thousand others, Moon? "Never want?" You should add: "Because you call the tune." And it isn't the old standard we've all been hearing is it? I believe that one belongs to Cross.'

Nick was fighting a real battle here, but he thought he detected an impatient sigh of annoyance.

'Well, well,' Nick added, 'Cross is singing out loud, and it bothers you, doesn't it? He doesn't like what you're doing, Moon, because you are keeping him from his own… what's the word? Ah yes, destiny?'

The figure moved, the shadows clinging to him. 'A sweet revenge, Tyler, because I'll be hanged if the devil himself is going to own Tibb's Cove.'

A scream, high, long and keening, fetched Tyler round. He ran down the rows, searching… searching for…

… a struggling Jane and someone he could only describe as the personification of everything unholy.

Purdy was running too, his waddling gait humorous in any other circumstances. He ran towards someone whom he knew must be the seventh man — the one in shadow, he of the burning eyes and widow's peak, the one from Emmy's stories, the very same who had scared Jerry and all the children down the centuries — the Very Reverend Mr. Black, the chief juggler, the laughing clown, the engineer… the one whose face was on the key ring.

'We've met. Mister Purdy. In a church I recall. You couldn't do anything then, and you're still frightened now.' The voice was grated ice.

Beyond them, the bombs were being loaded, ghost crew forging ahead on trailers. Jane screamed again.

Jerry's mind raced. If he couldn't do it by fire, then maybe supernatural heat would set things right. He was guessing, and he knew it, but he had to try. Again.

(How do you burn the devil?)

The thought was momentary: Purdy must go for it. He had to… to redeem himself.

He hurtled towards the levers, the switches, the dials, the ones Tom Sheridan had told him about in their weekly chats in the seafood stall. The order of their switching was paramount.

The Black thing's face was pure hatred, and powerful rage. Claws contorted through shredded gloves, yellow nails snagging the air.

Purdy flicked the switches, spun the dials, and an instantaneous combustion welded the metal structure, the heat tremendous.

'Have it all, you evil toad. TAKE IT BACK TO HELL.'

Purdy grabbed Jane. And the clown still laughed.

Moon stalked Tyler, Nick dodging between screens frantically trying to discover the source of their power. Like two children playing a game, Franklyn Moon feinted one way and then narrowly missed Tyler as he dodged the other.

'A lesser demon with pretensions, is it?' Tyler's taunts butting against the cold wall. A soft muted hiss of air told him something. He saw the vents. Air conditioning. All these screens reliant on constant temperature. If he could only...

Outside, the temperature climbed to dangerous levels.

In 1954 it had been an accident: they had meddled with things which didn't concern them. The machinery had looked old, unused. A switch clicked on here and there, a dial turned full up, and their laughter had turned to shock when the whole shebang burst into flame. They'd enjoyed it, him and Dykes, and they had destroyed — or thought they had — the demon in the flying suit from Emmy's tales.

The sea had bubbled, the mist had enveloped the shame of an experiment gone wrong, and then Moon had recaptured it, brought it back, brought them all back.

And Jerry recollected that something had flown across the moon.

Not a plane, but as he now knew, something far, far worse. The phrase *Fallen Angel* popped into his head.

Tyler shot through the door as bone white fingers raked his leather coat. He yelled as nails scored his skin and he hit the doors hard. Wood ruptured, one door askew, torn from its hinges.

Warmer air rushed in, hotter still when Tyler opened the front door...

Inside, screens ruptured, every face captured there running like melted plastic, as outside a grim reality destroyed Tibb's Cove, and the trauma which had held it.

Jerry Purdy did not understand. Why weren't they all dead?

Frank Sheridan still held his hammer above the bomber sitting on the table.

Thinking was for later:
  Nick Tyler thought...
  Jerry Purdy thought...
  They were alive. *Keep the thought.*
  Wanting and truth countermanded possession, and the thing wearing Gavin's body reshaped itself into Melville Cross, alongside a fleeting glimpse of Reverend Black. The power of merging souls — of demons.
  One and the same. The battle, as yet unfinished, would be threefold: the dead; the physical and the metaphysical.
  Ghost; human, and already damned.

The roar of the Lancaster's engine became a threat, and Jerry's yell propelled Jane towards the plane. 'RUN. IT'S OUR ONLY CHANCE.'
  The demon came about, indecision alive on its corrupt features, the blazing, pin prick eyes a revelation of its true self — The *true* Keeper of Souls as designated by His Satanic

Majesty.

GRUMPY taxied. 'GRAB THE LADDER,' Purdy urged, and he grabbed it for her. They ran with it. In the hangar, sparks blew from the dials, the inside of its vast dome a vivid, incandescent glow. Jane could feel her back blistering.

'PURDYYYY!' It was a cry from darkness, from the dreams he'd courted, the cadence rising, the remains of gloves flaking, as claws reached. It moved at breakneck speed, in its wake the things from the mist, all dressed in flying gear — the crews come back for their imprisoned souls now released by Tyler's action.

And it was what the demon wanted.

Purdy manhandled Jane into the plane and scrambled after her.

On the lane, the others looked on, the twins dancing in glee, Tom struggling to contain their evil. 'LET IT GO,' he demanded.

Len and Jaqui stayed behind the tree and prayed. Jaqui for Purdy, and Len for the wife who had brought about this evil through her stories, and through her belief in things she could not leave alone. And they prayed for a town no longer able to sustain life.

The dead had run their course, and without souls could no longer be alive.

The sign tilted; the fences leaned, wire snapped, pinging into the strange night. The cottage crumbled, ivy burned, glass imploded, and from inside, a new born soul screamed as Mattie Wells dashed in through the door, collected it and ran out towards the taxiing bomber.

And through the buckled gates of Hatcher's Field, in the lee of worm-eaten Nissen huts from where once pot-bellied stoves paid homage to boiling coffee pots, hell came into its own.

'"Curiouser and curiouser, said Alice",' Mattie intoned as she stood facing the aeroplane bearing down upon her.

And death sat in the cockpit dressed in a flying helmet and goggles, black eyes blazing as Mattie held up the wriggling bundle.

The demon reached out, and she welcomed it. She *was* Emily now, her own soul reborn as she embraced the darkness. Even as she cried out: 'I kept it warm for you, Mel,' she was engulfed, her charred remains left to smoulder on the ground.

In the Purdy house something stirred by the wardrobe: it wore air force blues, and if one studied it very closely, they would see it resembled a smiling photograph lying shattered on the floor.

But he would wait: wait for his son to come back. And forgive him for burying him under the azaleas.

GRUMPY headed over the trees, Purdy negotiating the narrow fuselage. The mid-upper gun turret was empty, the navigator's desk a mess of sodden charts. In the cabin, the joystick moved of its own volition.

'Where are they, Jerry?' Jane yelled above the racket. 'Where are the crew?'

Grunting and straining, Purdy squeezed his bulk into the narrow seat. He grabbed the stick. 'I'll show you who's a coward, George.'

The plane banked, the engines stuttering, screaming, props mashing the air, mincing the fog, GRUMPY refusing to respond to Jerry's efforts because... *something else held the stick.*

Purdy was incensed. 'GODDAMN YOU, FLY STRAIGHT TO HELL.'

And in a quiet suburban street, in a quiet suburban house, Frank Sheridan brought down his hammer —

— the tail sheered off sending GRUMPY into an erratic dive. Purdy fought with the controls, but couldn't master the thing which fought back, or the forces of nature.

The hammer fell once more, a wing tip flew through —

— the air, the wreckage scattered. And Purdy helped Jane buckle on a parachute, even as he shrugged into another. 'THEY'RE OLD,' he yelled above the noise, Jane able to accept the chance she must take, and its possible outcome. What other choice had they?

The hammer fell a third time, Frank stating: 'One for Marie; one for Johnny; and one for Dad.'

The bomber looped, tail-less, wingless, the giant coffin plummeted. With a full payload, it exploded on impact, destroying the hangar and everything in it, a vast fireball thrown out, razing everything within a four mile radius, a smoke plume spiralled ever higher.

The wind which followed scoured and cleansed, dust swirled, the fire purged. Gouts of flame reached from the fissures, then died, the holes closing, Hatcher's Field an empty, charred mass of nothing.

Beneath Madame Zara's sign, his face scalded by its glow, his breath ragged from his nightmare run, Nick Tyler knew he had both won and lost. He gave a resigned smile and turned up the street.

From an alleyway a dog barked, and O'Leary approached him with caution.

'Hey, fella.' Nick knelt. O'Leary backed away, a muffled bark there and gone, his hackles up. Then he turned and loped off.

'Suit yourself, Dog.'

Jane Lennard sat on the beach by the cave beneath Macey's Nose, the parachute drifting lazily across the rock pools. She cried for Purdy. The crazy sod had pushed her out, his words lost to her in the sudden rush of air.

Her wrist hurt, her back felt on fire, but she was okay, and able to pick her way slowly towards the dead town.

AFTERMATH

The charred sign was barely legible in the twilight. **Visit a real airfield** it said, and Len Wells sneered as he gazed over the silence that was Tibb's Cove.

It was 1996.

The monument erected on the lane close to where once the gates of Hatcher's Field had stood sported a weathered brass plaque.

**IN MEMORIAM
TO THE PEOPLE OF TIBB'S COVE
WHO LOST THEIR LIVES IN THE
TRAGIC ACCIDENT
JUNE 19TH, 1954**

And someone had scrawled underneath that date: *AND 1989.*

Hung across the stone was a cracked leather key fob, on it the face of the demon. Someone had set flowers. They were withered.

Len joined the others; Jaqui, Tom, Frank, Johnny and Charlie. A black dog sat close to the memorial.

By the breakwater, the girl stared out to sea, a piece of

ragged parachute — not hers — clenched tightly in her fist. She'd found it in August, 1989.

The tide raced in, but there were no footprints to wash away.

And in Moon's derelict factory off the Old Shore Road a light burned, as long, ragged fingers tapped computer keys. The graphics were rebuilding, remodelling, restoring the town and everyone in it...

For none may depart: how could they without their souls?

And the Devil who wore Nick Tyler's face laughed like a demented clown.

RAWHEAD & BLOODY BONES
and
ELUSIVE PLATO
Rhys H. Hughes

RAWHEAD AND BLOODY BONES — the story of two
dead entertainers and their tour of Europe.

ELUSIVE PLATO — the story of a lesbian trapped in a
man's body and his/her search for real love.

A magical blend of surreal fantasy, grotesque imagery,
bizarre characters and strange humour.

ISBN 190153006X — Price £6.99

EYELIDIAD

Rhys H. Hughes

Baron Darktree is a highwayman searching for gold he buried when he was younger. It's bad enough he has to put up with insults from his younger self (now a portrait he carries on his back), and that the map tattooed on his eyelid is no longer visible, but when he gets mistaken for Beer'or, the pagan god of golden beer, he begins to wonder how bad things can get.
Oh, much worse . . .

ISBN 0952718324 – Price £5.99

"Richly and hilariously imaginative, teeming with memorable images, and inimitably Welsh"
Ramsey Campbell

"the jaded fantasy reader will find much to enjoy here"
Flickers 'n' Frames

"imaginative slice of surrealist fantasy"
Samhain

SCAREMONGERS

It will take a brave man or woman to read through this
collection in one sitting. Each story needs a deep breath
before starting and a moment of reflection on completion.
All your fears are here and if you remain umoved by the end
- you must already be *dead*.
Not for the faint-hearted.

A collection of short stories from some of the big names in
horror — Ramsey Campbell, Ray Bradbury,
Michael Marshall Smith, Simon Clark, Mark Chadbourn,
Stephen Laws, Poppy Z. Brite, Stephen Gallagher, Dennis
Etchison, Freda Warrington, Steve Harris, Ben Leech, Peter
Crowther, Nicholas Royle and many more.
All royalties donated to Animal Welfare Charities

ISBN 1901530078 — Price £6.99

"Only seven quid to frighten the crap out of yourself on a
long winter night AND help some unwell cuddly bunnies at
the same time . . . Get this book now!" - *SFX*

"Scare yourself silly." - *The Big Issue*

"Excellent." - *Dragon's Breath*

MESMER

Tim Lebbon

When Rick sees his ex-girlfriend at a motorway service station he knows he must be losing his mind. For Penny had been brutally murdered and left to rot in a ditch eight years earlier. In trying to find answers to insane questions Rick finds himself immersed in a world where the dead can live again, a world controlled by the evil powers of the Mesmer.

ISBN 1901530027 – Price £5.99

"Mesmer is absolutely superb. Lebbon's going to be big one day. Start reading him now."
Simon Clark

"Mesmer is an excellent taster from a new writer." - *SFX*

"a firm and confident style, with elements of early Clive Barker" - *Phil Rickman, Radio Wales*

"Mesmer is beautifully written, with Lebbon timing the fireworks to perfection" - *Zene*

RECLUSE

Derek M. Fox

A letter from a mysterious woman is all it takes to turn Daniel Lees's world upside-down. He suspects his wife of having an affair. He believes his children are in danger from something that stalks the moors. He is haunted by a past that will not leave him alone.

Finally he has to face up to what he really is and battle against the nightmare that has threatened to destroy everything he holds dear.

ISBN 1901530000 – Price £5.99

"*Recluse* is the chilling journey into the heart of a nightmare. Reader beware – Derek M. Fox is set to be a new Master of Fear."
Mark Chadbourn

"maintaining a cracking pace and an iron grip on the reader's attention."
BBR Directory

SCATTERED REMAINS

Paul Pinn

A collection of short stories to celebrate the 750th anniversary of the Bethlem Mental Hospital, the origin of the word bedlam. Each story is an examination of mental illness within the dark underbelly of human nature. Make sure you read this with the lights on.

ISBN 1901530051 – Price £6.99

"Soul-searing . . . totally bleak, remorseless and nihilistic."
Pam Creais, Dementia 13

"Black, claustrophobic, full of dirt and death . . . I like it."
Dave Logan, Grotesque Magazine

"A fine - and very disturbing - collection"- *SFX*

"Get into him now and let the nightmares begin"
'Blood from Stones', Waterstones Newsletter

PRISONERS OF LIMBO

David Ratcliffe

When the Carter family move to the new estate they hope it
will mean the end of their troubles. Tommy Carter is never
out of trouble, and Lucy Carter has a weakness for bad men.
These hopes are soon dashed when they discover they are
the only residents and the estate is half-finished.
It soon becomes clear that somehow they have passed
through a barrier of normality. In this world the dead are
alive, the past is the present, and everything is in
monochrome.
The problem is how to escape and return to the *real* world
before it's too late.

ISBN 1901530043 – Price £5.99

"A dark, dirty tale – horror noir at its finest."
Night Dreams

"Outer Limits-on-speed, Timeslip-on-acid."
Dragon's Breath

THE ENGINEER

Neal L. Asher

They moved suns and on some worlds were worshipped as gods. They had been gone from the galaxy for five million years. Then the science vessel Schrodinger's Box discovers one drifting through deepest space...
But not everyone shares the scientists' joy.

Also included six short stories from the master of science fiction horror.

ISBN 1901530086 — Price £6.99

THE DISAFFECTED

Ceri Jordan

Crow has been implanted with millions of pounds worth of cybernetic enhancements. But like a lot of teenagers he just wants to rebel. Crow is special. Running away from home is not going to be easy. Not with hired killers on his trail, and the authorities trying to bring him back in.

And who owns the mysterious voice that buzzes in his head? Someone who wants to use Crow's unique abilities for his own purpose.

**THE YOUNG ALWAYS REBEL
BUT NEVER LIKE THIS**

ISBN 1901530094 – Price £6.99

SCAREMONGERS 2:
Redbrick Eden

Amongst the rubble that is England, where there is no shelter, where hope is a dim and distant memory, where every day is a struggle to survive, where despair is king, here, there is HORROR

A COLLECTION OF SHORT STORIES IN AID OF SHELTER

featuring: Keith Brooke, Ramsey Campbell, Mark Chadbourn, Simon Clark, Mary Corran, Peter Crowther, Christopher Fowler, Steve Harris, Joel Lane, Stephen Laws, Tim Lebbon, Ben Leech, Paul Lewis, Steve Lockley, Simon Morden, Mark Morris, Kim Newman, Nicholas Royle, Gavin Williams
edited by Steve Savile

ISBN 1901530140 – Price £6.99